THE WIZARD IN THE WOOD

LOUIE STOWELL

illustrated by
DAVIDE ORTU

Walker Books

Text copyright © 2021 by Louie Stowell
Illustrations copyright © 2021 by Davide Ortu

First US edition 2022
First published by Nosy Crow (UK) 2021

Library of Congress Catalog Card Number 2021947325
ISBN 978-1-5362-1495-6 (hardcover)
ISBN 978-1-5362-2423-8 (paperback)

22 23 24 25 26 27 LBM 10 9 8 7 6 5 4 3 2 1

Printed in Melrose Park, IL, USA

This book was typeset in Chaparral Pro.
The illustrations were created digitally.

Walker Books US
a division of
Candlewick Press
99 Dover Street
Somerville, Massachusetts 02144

www.walkerbooksus.com

To Gus,
the youngest wizard
in the world

LS

This is Josh's notebook.

Kit and Alita, if you mess with it, I will know. I have records of your fingerprints, so I will be able to dust the cover for prints.

You have been warned. I have read a lot of detective novels, so I know all the tricks.

Dear Future Josh,

In case an evil future wizard has done a mindwipe spell on you, here are some notes about what happened this summer. Spoiler: it was INTENSE with a capital everything!

1. We discovered that our local librarian, Faith, is a wizard and my friend Kit is one, too.

2. We found out that a dragon sleeps beneath the library, and it's a wizard's duty to keep it asleep.

3. Our local library was attacked by an evil businessman who wanted to wake up the dragon.

4. We beat him, because we are an incredible team of magical library protectors.

5. Then, later in the summer,
Kit's magic started going wrong.

6. We tracked down the source of
her problems: there was a monster
in the lake in our local park! It
had been kicked out of its home
in Scotland by evil mermaids.

7. We went to Scotland to talk
to the mermaids. It turns out
they weren't evil . . . they were
being controlled by evil ghost
rats from the dawn of time!

8. Kit did a big spell with some help
from me and Alita. We beat the evil
ghost rats and freed the mermaids.

9. The mermaids still weren't very
nice, but the lake monster was
able to go home and everything

went back to normal. Well, sort
of. Our lives are still very weird.

I think that's it. But every day I'm
finding out more about the world of
magic! I wonder what I'll find out
today. Oh. Kit's telling me we have to go.

Yes we do. Come on. Don't be boring. LET'S
GO! Trees to climb! Worlds to save!
Kit

CHAPTER 1

JOSH'S LIFE FLASHES BEFORE HIS EYES

I cannot believe you talked me into doing this." Josh clung more tightly to the branch he and Kit were sitting on.

"It's what kids do in the summer," said Kit. "It's called fun. Look! There's a squirrel over there!" Kit stood up on the branch, causing it to shake and making Josh hold on even tighter.

"I don't call this fun," muttered Josh. "I call this terror. My life is flashing in front of my eyes. Wow," he added. "I did a lot of reading and ate some good jollof rice."

The first day of the new school year was only a few days away, and Kit wanted to milk every last moment of freedom. Josh was more focused on not crashing down from his perch and breaking every bone in his lanky body.

"The thing is," Josh said, "this isn't natural. Humans are not tree-dwelling creatures. We're supposed to be on the ground."

"Since when is being natural the only way to do things? If everything was natural, we'd all be living in caves," objected Kit.

"At least caves are on the ground," said Josh.

"Guys," called Alita from one of the lower branches, "stop arguing. Faith's coming down the path. She looks like she's in a hurry!"

Kit, Josh, and Alita scrambled down the tree to meet Faith. Josh scrambled a lot more slowly and carefully—he hadn't wanted to get his shoes dirty on the tree, so he was barefoot.

"Hi, Faith. Is everything OK?" Alita gasped. "Oh, no. Did Kit's mom tell my mom we went out instead of playing at home? Is she here? Is she mad?"

Faith smiled. "Everything's fine. I have good news, actually."

"What?" asked Josh, sitting down to put on his pure-white sneakers. "Has the new Danny Fandango book been released early?"

"Well, no, nothing *that* exciting," said Faith. "But the Wizards' Council wants to meet Kit. And they have a present."

"Oh?" said Kit. She wasn't exactly excited about meeting the Wizards' Council. Everything Faith had said about them made them sound very old and very grumpy. "What's the present?"

Faith motioned zipping her lips and waggled her eyebrows. "It's a surprise."

"Can we come and meet the Wizards' Council, too?" asked Josh.

"Sorry, no," said Faith. "The headquarters is a wizard-only zone." She shrugged. "Part of the whole secrecy-and-security thing."

"That's not fair," said Kit.

"Have I ever accused the Wizards' Council of being fair?" asked Faith.

"I don't mind," said Alita. "I want to spend as much time as I can with Dogon!" Dogon was the furry, scaly creature who lived beneath the library: half dog, half dragon, and always hungry. "I've hardly seen him in days because of my auntie's wedding. I thought it would never end!" She splayed her hands, showing the intricate henna designs on her palms. "I'm going to miss him so much when I go back to school."

"He's going to miss the snacks you bring him, that's for sure." Faith laughed. She turned to Josh. "Why don't you go and read to Draca?"

Draca was the dragon who slept beneath Chatsworth Library, and like all dragons, she didn't belong in the waking world. Instead, she wandered through her own dreams, made up of the stories that were read to her as she slumbered through the years.

"Perhaps you could start a new book?" suggested Faith.

Josh's eyes lit up with pure excitement, as though Faith had just offered him a ride through space on a unicorn.

"Oh, yes! I can read her some poetry. I don't think I've read her any of that before!"

"How are we getting to the Wizards' Council?" asked Kit.

"From the library," said Faith. "So let's all head there now. One last time before school starts."

THE NEW PORTAL BOOK

CHAPTER 2

Kit, Josh, Alita, and Faith walked through Chatsworth Library toward the stacks—the hidden parts of the building that the general public never got to see. The parts where the magic lay hidden and where Draca slept and dreamed of stories.

They reached a shelf at the back of the library, and Faith checked to see that no other people were near, then pulled on a book and murmured, *"Labba."* The whole shelf of books slid to one side to reveal a door that led down into darkness.

Faith tapped herself on the forehead and breathed, *"Ina!"* A ball of light appeared in the corridor ahead, lighting their way and revealing shelves of books on either side of the passage.

The four of them walked down and down into the darkness, until the passage widened and lightened and became an open green space. They were in the Book Wood again. Each tree in this forest had once been a book, and if you looked closely enough at the papery green page-leaves, you could make out faint letters. Kit inhaled deeply. The air smelled of leaves and flowers and secondhand books.

"I'll go find Dogon!" said Alita.

"And I'll read Draca these poems," said Josh, holding up the book he'd brought with him from the library upstairs.

"So how exactly are we getting to the Wizards' Council?" asked Kit. "Are we going to use a portal book?"

Portal books were the main magical way to travel between libraries. To use one, you simply began reading out loud, and the magic sucked you into the world of the book. When you reached the end, you spoke the name of the library you wanted to reach, and you

reappeared in the real world again. Some of these books were safer than others.

"I thought we'd take a stroll through a new portal book this time," said Faith.

"A new one?" That sparked Kit's interest. "I didn't know there *were* new ones."

"Oh, yes, from time to time," said Faith. "I made this one just for you. It should be just about ripe . . ."

Faith took a few steps, then pointed up at the branches of a tree. Hanging like a fruit among the page-leaves was a book. On the cover it said *Super Magic Quest*, with a picture of a cartoon rabbit wearing armor, and a goblin by its side.

"Pick it," said Faith. "It's ready."

Kit reached out and took hold of the bottom

of the book. With the gentlest of tugs, it came away from the tree in her hand. She turned the book over. "How did you make this?"

"I planted an ordinary copy of the book when you first became a wizard," said Faith. "It's taken the past month for this tree to grow. Draca put extra effort into sharing her magic with it, so it would be ready for you when you needed it."

"That's so nice of her!" said Kit. Draca was a strange creature, but she could be very kind at times.

"We both thought you might enjoy a portal book that wasn't dangerous, but was still fun," said Faith.

"Ooh! It's a comic!" said Kit as she opened it.

"It's about a rabbit on a quest in a magical land," said Faith. "I believe there's a forest made of Jell-O in there somewhere."

"Sounds really silly. I love it already!" said Kit. She sat on the ground and started to read the comic. On the first page, a rabbit called Jorril was setting out on a quest to find a magic gem . . .

Without warning, Kit and Faith were inside the pages of the book.

After a perilous journey through a desert full of tiny flying bears and a fight with a giant robot made of glue, they finally reached the end of Jorril's quest.

"*Council, hus!*" said Faith, wiping robo-glue out of her eye. They left the book with a *pop* and appeared in the library of the Wizards' Council.

CHAPTER 3

THE COUNCIL

Kit and Faith were in a huge, rectangular room with rough stone walls. Bookshelves were stacked from the floor to the lofty ceiling, holding more books than Kit had ever seen before. In between the bookshelves were windows filled with stained glass. One showed a picture of a dragon cowering beneath a shower of glowing yellow sparks. Another showed a dragon and a wizard, hand in claw, gazing out from the glass in dozens of colors.

"Welcome to the council library," said Faith.

Kit gazed around in awe. It was like a gigantic church, but for books.

"I imagine someone from the council will be here in a minute," said Faith. "They knew we were coming, but it sometimes takes them a while to get upstairs. They're not as young as they used to be, and they were already old then."

Spaced around the carpeted floor were comfy, battered armchairs and little tables littered with abandoned cups of tea and candy wrappers.

A moment later there was a creaking sound, and a bookshelf swung open to reveal a dark corridor behind it. Out came a tall, broad-shouldered white woman with white hair and a green pantsuit, with a green flower in her lapel. Kit couldn't tell how old she was, but definitely old enough for her birthday candles to be a fire hazard. The woman's eyes seemed to look off into the distance, while also somehow boring straight into Kit's soul. Kit felt a sudden urge to stand up straighter, and maybe clean her bedroom.

"That's the chairwizard," whispered Faith. "Branwen Williams."

"Faith Braithwaite!" said the older woman. Her

voice had a lilt to it. "Kit Spencer! This way! The council is ready for you." She beckoned them to the opening in the wall.

Just like under Chatsworth Library, the tunnel was lined with books, but this one was much, much bigger. You could have driven a train through it. A double-decker train, with a couple of spies having a dramatic fight on top of it.

A green glow appeared in the tunnel ahead. Kit got a shivery feeling of powerful magic. She felt a little like that in the wood beneath Chatsworth Library, but this was different. It was like the difference between being tickled with a feather and jumping into a swimming pool full of wriggly snakes. Her whole body felt as though it were bursting with light.

Then she saw the wood.

"Oh!"

She'd never seen anything like it. A lump formed in her throat. It was beautiful. The view, not the lump.

Branwen stopped and gestured around. "Ah, yes.

I forget what it must be like to see it for the first time. Quite a sight, isn't it?"

The trees seemed to stretch forever under a curving greenish sky. There were firs and oaks, chestnut trees and little blossoming apple trees, all with leaves that once were pages, and trunks carved with spells. There were huge ancient trees and brand-new shoots, and everywhere there was a gentle breeze and the sound of ruffling pages.

"Where are we meeting the others?" asked Faith.

Branwen pointed to a tree nearby. "Downstairs."

Faith's eyes lit up. "You're going to love this, Kit."

As Branwen approached, a door opened in the tree, just like the door that led down to Draca's lair back home.

The magical, thrumming excitement inside Kit grew.

"Are we going to see the dragon?" she asked.

"Yes," said Branwen as she began to climb slowly down the spiral stairs inside the tree. "But more importantly, she's going to see *you*. I respect her opinion highly, mind you."

They climbed down for a long time. Kit's mind wandered as she took painfully slow steps behind the older wizard.

"How many wizards are there on the council?" she asked Faith.

"Seven," said Faith. "Well. There are seven council members. Six of them are wizards."

"Wow, so they allow non-wizards on the council?" asked Kit.

"You'll find out," said Branwen. "Always in a hurry, the young. You wouldn't be in such a hurry if you knew how fast time flies."

Kit thought that was typical. Old people loved giving advice on how to be young. She didn't go around giving advice about being old, did she?

As they reached the bottom of the staircase, they came to a pair of doors that looked like they belonged on a castle. They opened as Branwen approached.

In the stone chamber beyond the doors, Kit saw exactly what she had been hoping to see. A dragon.

Huge and red, with vast folded wings and puffs of smoke emerging from its spiky nostrils.

Around the dragon stood a group of elderly men and women, all wearing blue cloaks.

"This is Edith, Iyesha, Kwame, Gladys, and Duc," said Branwen, gesturing unhelpfully toward all of them.

"I'm Edith," said a pale woman with thin gray hair, who leaned on a stick.

"Iyesha," said a friendly woman with a round face and a bright sari. "Welcome, Kit and Faith. I hope your journey wasn't too hard?"

"There was a lot of Jell-O," said Kit, feeling shy and awkward.

"Ready? Then we'll begin," said Branwen.

And then, as they all touched the dragon's scales, everything went black.

CHAPTER 4

THE POOL OF FIRE

And just like that, Kit, Faith, and the council were inside the dragon's dream. The wizards found themselves sitting in ornate chairs around a circular table. The dragon sat with them, currently human-size.

"Kit, this is Draig," said Branwen, "the seventh member of our council." She gestured at the dragon.

Ohhhh, thought Kit. *That kind of non-wizard!*

Draig bowed her head. "A pleasure to meet you, little one."

"Hello, Draig," said Kit. She felt very shy all of a sudden. She didn't like being surrounded by so many imposing grown-ups in such a formal place.

"Thank you for having us here," said Faith, nudging Kit.

"Yes, thank you!" said Kit.

"Do have some tea," said Draig.

Cups of tea appeared on the table in front of them, along with a plate of buns with raisins, and some sticky orange sweets.

Iyesha piled a heap of them onto her plate before passing them down the table. "Mmmm," she said. "Jalebi! Thank you, Draig!"

"We're here for something very special," said Branwen. "A moment that only happens once every century or so. This is only the second time I have ever witnessed it myself."

How old is she? Kit wondered. She was very grateful that she didn't say it out loud, until she realized that the dragon would be able to hear her thoughts. But Draig didn't give her away. She merely waggled her scaly brows.

The wizards all held hands around the table.

Faith took Kit's, and Kit held the dry, wrinkly hand of the wizard beside her.

Kit heard a low rumbling from all around them. It grew gradually louder and turned into a kind of music. Not the kind you get from instruments, but something like the sound of a storm, turned into beautiful melodies and thundering beats. Kit held her breath. The stone table where they were sitting began to change. The tea and sweets were gone. They were all on their feet, with no chairs in sight.

Now they were in a wild wood, standing around a dark pool by moonlight. The surface of the pool rippled, sending circles out from the center. The dark water grew lighter and redder, and suddenly the pool was made of fire. Flames licked up from the surface, and Kit felt the urge to jump back, but her hands were held tightly. She looked up at Faith, who nodded to her, as though to say, *Everything's OK.*

Everything is OK, Kit told herself. But something was coming.

The dragon, Draig, had closed her eyes. Even within the dream she seemed to be going deeper into her own world. She started to hum, a low sound that joined with the rumbling. Then, out of the pool of fire rose a shape, like a giant football.

No, not a ball. An egg.

Draig reached for it. She held it up in her claws for everyone to see. Her smile spread wide and sharp. Her eyes flashed. "It is done!" she said in the lowest of purrs.

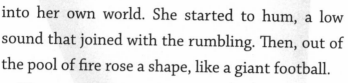

"Congratulations!" said one of the council members. He held up an imaginary glass in a *cheers* gesture. As he did so, the glass appeared and he drained it.

"Is that what I think it is?" asked Kit, pointing at the egg.

"If you think it's a dragon's egg, then yes," said Faith.

"So dragons are born from pools of fire inside a dream?" Kit's brain was boggling.

"How else did you think they'd be born?" asked Branwen. "In a hospital?"

"No, but maybe I thought it would come . . . out of a dragon?" said Kit, looking at Draig in embarrassment.

"We're not farm chickens," said Draig. "We're ancient magical beings from before the dawn of time." She held out the egg to Kit. "Now. Take the little one to its new home. Goodbye."

"Goodbye." The six wizards spoke as one, and then disappeared from the dragon's dream.

"Goodbye," said Kit and Faith.

And everything went black again.

CHAPTER 5

HOW TO RAISE AN EGG

Back in the dragon's chamber, Kit was holding the egg out in front of her. It was bigger than any egg she had ever seen, and slightly reddish. It was also heavy. She put it down, ever so carefully.

"Should we put it under the dragon to hatch?" Kit whispered to Faith.

Faith shook her head. "She's not a chicken, remember? For a dragon egg to hatch, you need to lay it beneath its own library. It's a bit like planting a seed. You speak a spell over the egg, and it sinks down into the earth, making its own cavern. After a few days, the egg hatches."

Kit imagined the egg on the floor cracking and hatching. What would the little dragon inside look like? She couldn't wait to find out.

"Where's this egg's library?" asked Kit. Her mind was racing with questions.

"Not far from ours," said Faith. "The exact location is a surprise."

Kit narrowed her eyes.

"A good surprise," said Faith, laughing.

"How's it getting there?" asked Kit. "To its new library. Can we go with it?"

"Of course you can—you're taking it," said Branwen. "Honestly, you're a bit clueless, aren't you? I would've thought wild magic might have chosen a slightly cleverer child as the youngest wizard in the world."

That stung.

"So . . . " said Faith. "We'd better take this to its new home! Let's head upstairs."

Kit started to feel nervous. What if she dropped the egg on her way back up?

Faith was watching her and smiled. "Don't worry. It's pretty tough. You could drop it down a hundred flights of stairs and it wouldn't break."

Kit carried it upstairs carefully all the same, with Branwen walking behind.

In the library above, Branwen gave Kit a stern warning. "It might be physically tough, but it's vulnerable to magic," she said. "And you never know who might try to take it from you. Take good care."

Just then, a bell rang. Branwen sighed. "No rest for the ancient," she said to Kit and Faith. "You can show yourselves out."

Faith nodded, and Branwen disappeared down the corridor and back to the Book Wood.

"Start reading," suggested Faith, picking up the portal book they'd used to get there. "I'll hold on to the egg while we're entering a magical space."

So Kit began to read the comic, and moments later, the library was gone.

When they reappeared in the library at the other end, there was no one around. Faith found a box for them to put the egg in. "So it's a surprise for Alita and Josh," she said.

They found the others down in Draca's lair, with Dogon curled up on Alita's lap as she drew a sketch of Draca, and Josh reading a very long book to the dragon.

Josh stopped reading as they came in. "How was the council?"

"We brought you back a present," said Kit.

"Present!" said Alita, dropping her sketchbook and scurrying over, sending Dogon fluttering up grumpily into the air.

"Is it a spell book?" asked Josh, eyeing the box.

"Is it a cake?" asked Alita.

"Come on," said Kit. "Do you think the Wizards' Council would trust me with a cake? It would be eaten by the time we got through the portal book. Open it!" She couldn't wait to see their faces.

Alita pried open a tiny edge of the box, then

slowly, slowly lifted it up. Then she lifted the next flap up, just as slowly.

This was almost as bad as watching her eat a chocolate bar piece by piece.

Josh noticed Kit's impatience. "It's called delayed gratification," he said. "Which is when you put off doing something nice so it'll be nicer when it comes."

Kit shook her head. "No it won't. It just means more time without the nice thing."

But when Alita finally opened the lid of the box and peered inside, her face showed a kind of joy that Kit couldn't even imagine feeling, not even after climbing the highest tree in the world. Like sunlight was shining out of her dark-brown eyes.

Josh peered into the box, and his face almost matched hers. "Is that what I think it is?" he asked in a small voice.

"A dragon's egg!" breathed Alita. "A real dragon's egg!"

"And it's ours!" said Kit triumphantly.

"No!" said Faith.

The children looked at her quizzically.

"It's yours to help care for. But a dragon only ever belongs to itself," said Faith.

"So we get to care for it?" asked Alita. "This is the best thing to happen since I met Dogon!"

Faith nodded. "It will live beneath a library close by, so you can visit it often."

Alita would have jumped up and down if she hadn't been cradling the egg like a baby. She did, however, let out an excited sound somewhere between a cat mewing and a kettle boiling.

"If you're this excited about an egg, I'm worried you're going to literally explode when it hatches into a dragon," Kit said, laughing.

"It'll be worth it!" said Alita.

"More importantly," said Josh, "is there a book on caring for dragon eggs?"

"There are hundreds," said Faith. "I'll show you later. But first, we need to plant the egg. Follow me."

The children followed her, with a million questions, up away from Draca's lair and through the Book Wood. Dogon followed them, flapping close to Alita and snuffling at the dragon's egg.

"Get off! You might make me drop it! That's, like, your cousin or something in there!" said Alita, batting the creature away.

Dogon growled at the egg.

"I think he's jealous!" said Kit.

"Silly Dogon," said Alita. "I can love you *and* a baby dragon at the same time."

"When will the egg hatch?" Josh asked Faith.

"Soon," said Faith. "In a few days."

"Shouldn't we be putting it under the dragon to hatch?" asked Alita.

"Dragons aren't chickens, you know," said Kit, feeling very wise. "They don't lay eggs out of their bottoms. This egg came out of a pool of fire. We're going to bury it beneath a library, speak a spell over it, and it'll sink down and down to make its own cavern. Then it'll hatch." She beamed at them proudly.

Alita and Josh did a double take, unused to Kit knowing more than them. It didn't last long, though.

"How big is the dragon going to be when it hatches?" asked Josh. "Which library are we burying it under?"

"When it hatches, will it already be asleep?" asked Alita. "What does it eat?"

"Uh . . . " said Kit.

"Wait and see," said Faith. "Weren't you just telling Kit about delayed gratification?"

"I hate it when people use my own arguments against me," muttered Josh.

"Kit, we're going in there," said Faith, pointing at a tree in the Book Wood. "Use the *moria* spell I taught you the other day to open a tunnel. I've already enchanted the tree to guide the tunnel's path."

Kit nodded and spoke the spell carefully. *"Moria beneath us open. Hollow stollen down ididay."*

A circle of the tree's bark melted away, creating a dark doorway. Kit went in first, carrying the egg into the darkness.

"Ina!" she said, tapping her own forehead. A ball of light appeared ahead of them, and they started off down a flight of stairs, which changed into a winding pathway that seemed to be made of hard-packed earth. It smelled a little damp, but also alive.

"Where are we going?" asked Josh.

"Wait and see," said Faith.

Kit felt the anticipation building. She had no idea where they could be by now. They couldn't be under the library anymore. They'd walked too far. But she didn't know of any other libraries nearby.

The small light spell she'd cast only showed a few feet around them, but the drop in temperature and a change in the smell of the air told Kit they were in a larger space now.

"Ina vyaapak!" said Faith in an echoing voice.

Light blazed out from the tips of her fingers, showing that they were standing in an enormous cavern. The floor was mossy and the walls were covered in shelves full of books. More books were scattered on the mossy ground. Dogon flew over to sniff them, swooping up and down, then flying up high and doing a loop the loop.

"What happened here?" asked Kit. "Who threw all those books on the ground?"

"Me," said Faith. "But I didn't throw them. I planted them. This, Kit, is the beginning of a new Book Wood."

"It doesn't look like a wood," said Kit.

"Be patient," said Faith. "The forest can't begin to grow until the dragon egg has been planted."

"Where are we?" asked Josh.

Faith pointed upward with an elegantly nailed finger. "We're right below your school. This is where we're planting the egg."

"But you said the egg had to be planted beneath a library. We don't have a school library," said Kit.

"Yeah," said Alita. "I spent ages helping my mom campaign to get us one, so we can't have one already."

"Surprise!" said Faith. "The campaign worked! You have a library just above our heads!"

Josh and Alita looked like all their Christmases and Diwalis and birthdays had come at once. Even Kit felt at least Easter-levels of pleased. Sure, she didn't want more books in her life. But magic, beneath her school? That was worth something.

"I can't believe the campaign worked!" said Alita excitedly. "My mom didn't say a thing!"

"She wanted it to be a surprise when you got to school," said Faith. "So tell her you were surprised, all right?"

"I will look so surprised my eyes might almost fall out of my head," promised Alita. "She'll be calling the optometrist before I've finished being surprised!"

Faith chuckled. "Excellent! It should all be up and running on the first day of school—the Wizards' Council is sending a new librarian! Your mom even persuaded the parent-teacher association to help pay their salary. She might not be a wizard, but that counts as magic in my book!"

"Oh," said Josh. His face fell. "Aren't you going to be our librarian?"

"I can't manage more than one library at a time," said Faith. "The school deserves its own librarian, to give the books—and, once it's hatched, the dragon—all the care and attention they deserve."

"So who is going to be our librarian?" asked Kit.

"An old friend," said Faith with a smile. "You'll like him. His name's Ben Picarda. We went to the Wizard Academy together, but I haven't spoken to him in a while. He's been living on a remote island, practicing his magic until he got allocated his own library. Now, let's plant that egg!"

"We don't have to dig, do we?" asked Josh, poking the moss cautiously with his white sneaker.

Faith shook her head. "There's a spell for that." She gestured around at the cavern. "This is the beginning of the Book Wood. When we plant the egg, it will begin to flourish. And when the dragon hatches . . ." She trailed off. "Well, you'll see."

"What are we waiting for, then?" asked Kit. "Let's plant the egg!"

Faith nodded. "Say the spell after me. And raise your arms like this."

She raised her arms—both arms—wide and high.

Kit did the same.

Faith began to chant, one line at a time. Kit followed her, echoing her words.

Kit felt the magic build. It had a flavor to it, like fresh-mown grass and springtime. There was an aftertaste of metal, and a feeling of lightning under her skin. This was wild magic like she'd never felt before.

It felt amazing!

CHAPTER 6

THE BEGINNING OF THE WOOD

The ground beneath the egg sparkled and rippled. There was a faint rumbling beneath them, and the children took a step back.

Faith lowered her hands and stopped speaking. "Even farther back!" She shooed them closer to the edge of the cavern as the spell truly took hold.

The egg and the ground around it began to sink, sparkling as it went.

"The new dragon's chamber is forming," said Faith.

The sparkles around the egg started to take on solid shapes, forming a mound beneath the egg.

"Treasure!" Kit said with a gasp. She kneeled to

grab a fistful, but it slipped between her fingers like sand.

"It's not fully solid yet," said Faith. "Also, hands off! That belongs to the dragon."

"I just wanted to touch it," grumbled Kit.

"How would you like it if a dragon came and messed up your bed?" said Faith.

"I wouldn't mind. My bed is already as messy as it can be," said Kit, grinning.

Faith let out a deep, heartfelt sigh and massaged her temples.

"Why *do* dragons sleep on treasure?" asked Josh.

"Gold is good for their skin," said Faith. "Also, it's traditional."

The egg had sunk down out of sight now, and the glow was fading. Above the pit it had formed, the ground knitted itself back together, and soon it was as though nothing had ever been there.

"How do we get down there?" asked Alita. "To visit the egg?"

"The stairs will grow as soon as the first tree sprouts," said Faith. "And to grow the first tree, we need to read the egg its very first story. Would you like to go and pick one from the new library?"

"Yessss!" said Josh, making a fist of victory.

"Can Dogon come?" asked Alita. He fluttered down to land on her shoulder.

"Probably better if he doesn't. I don't want to have to explain any dragon droppings to Ben on his first day," said Faith.

"Go on home," said Alita to Dogon. "I'll see you later. I may even bring you a treat."

When Dogon heard the T-word, he was off in a blur of wings and scales.

Faith led them up another tunnel between two bookshelves in the wall of the cavern. It sloped gently upward until they reached a wall of books. Faith nudged one of them out of place, and the shelf slid sideways.

They were in an unfamiliar library, full of new books but no people.

Faith turned to them, arms folded, with a satisfied look on her face. "I do love that new-library smell."

Josh and Alita ran off through the shelves to see what treasures the new library held that they could read to the dragon's egg below.

"So," said Faith to Kit. "What do you think?"

"I can't believe I have *another* library to do shelving in," said Kit. But secretly, she was pleased.

"You love it, don't you?" said Faith with a smile.

"OK, I might like it. A bit," said Kit, unable to stop herself from smiling. She glanced around. "There aren't any teachers here yet, are there?" She didn't want to be caught on school premises and get a detention before the year even started.

"Don't worry. They're not here until tomorrow," said Faith. "We have the place to ourselves."

"We've got the perfect book!" said Alita, holding a book and pelting down between the shelves, with Josh just behind.

"*The Goose That Laid the Golden Egg*," said Josh.

"We thought the egg might like something it can relate to emotionally," Alita explained.

They went back down the way they had come. "It's this book that you pull out here," said Faith, pointing to a dusty old volume about ships. "The usual spell."

Kit pulled it and said the same spell that opened the stacks in the public library. *"Labba."*

Once they were down in the cavern, they sat on a rock together and Alita started reading. It didn't take long before a tiny green shoot sprouted out of one of the books that lay on the ground.

Josh was scribbling in his book and looking at his watch.

The shoot grew and grew, like a magical beanstalk—only, as it grew, it became coated in bark. It was a fully grown tree!

First shoot sprouted up as soon as Alita started reading! It looks a bit like this.

Then, one minute thirty-
five seconds later, it
looked like this.

Then, after
three minutes, it
looked like this.

"Wow," said Kit. "That was fast! And I'm not very
patient, so it must have been *really* fast."

"Three minutes," agreed Josh. "Well, three minutes thirty seconds if you count it sprouting flowers." He gestured to the fully grown tree, which was

now in full bloom. It looked like no tree Kit had ever climbed. Its bark had a slight golden shimmer to it, and the flowers were fluffy and white, like the feathers inside a very fancy pillow.

"It's awesome, isn't it?" said Kit to Alita.

Alita looked like she was about to cry. She did that when she was happy sometimes. Kit never really understood it.

"I made that happen," said Alita in a tiny voice.

"Yes, you did," said Faith, patting her on the shoulder.

Faith, Kit, and Alita took turns reading stories to the dragon after that, sitting in the Book Wood as it grew around them, or sometimes sitting beside the egg in its new cavern. They read the egg stories of dragons and baby birds and trains and rainy days and adventures in lands near and far.

They visited the egg multiple times that day and read it lots of stories. Each time they went down to visit, new shoots were growing above it in the Book Wood—the beginnings of lots of tiny trees. The children were thrilled.

"And that's nothing compared to what will happen to the wood once the dragon hatches," said Faith. They were heading down from the new wood to the dragon's lair, down the stairs that seemed to go on forever.

They reached the egg and crowded around it. Kit thought she heard something. A *tap-tap-tapping* sound.

It was coming from inside the egg.

"Is it going to hatch right now?" she asked, feeling a fizz of both magic and excitement flowing through her.

"Not yet," said Faith. She pulled out her thaumometer and held up the flute-like magical device, like someone using their wet finger to test the direction of the wind. The gem at its end glowed purple. "Soon!" she said with satisfaction. "And when it does, the hatching energy will give the wood an extra boost of growth to get it going. So, fingers crossed, next time you're down here—or rather, up there . . . "—she pointed above their heads, up to the new Book Wood—"you'll see so many trees. Unless you're lucky enough to be down here exactly when it hatches. Now . . . time to go home. School tomorrow!"

School, Kit thought, *and a brand-new baby dragon.*

She knew which one she was more excited about.

THE NEW LIBRARIAN

"Phew, we made it here before everyone else!" said Josh. The friends had gathered in the library before school to visit the dragon egg.

"I'm not sure anyone else was making a dash for the library on the first day of school," said Kit.

"Well, everyone else *should* rush here," said Josh with a sniff. "It's where the books are!"

"But the playground is where the climbing structure is," Kit pointed out.

"Shh! We're not alone," said Alita. She nudged Kit to the right.

A man was sitting behind the desk at the back

of the library, with his head in a big book. The three children approached him. He was skinny and white, with a lot of dark-brown hair sticking up in all directions, and blue eyes behind square-framed glasses. He wore a tweed jacket with elbow patches over an Anarchy T-shirt, and bright-green skinny pants.

"Hello?" said Kit, trying to get his attention.

He looked up with a start, almost dropping his book. "Sorry, I didn't notice you there. Deep in this." He held up the book. It was the first Danny Fandango.

"Ooh, what part are you up to?" asked Josh.

"I just met Lara Fandango's pet fox!" he said. "Now I want a pet fox."

"Me too!" said Alita. "Actually I want lots of pet foxes. Especially talking ones."

The man smiled, then turned his gaze to Kit. His blue eyes were intense behind his glasses. "So. Are you the young wizard I've heard so much about?"

"Shhh!" said Josh. "We're not supposed to say

the W-word in public!" He glanced around nervously, eyeing a couple of younger boys who'd just come into the library and had made a beeline for a few of the lower shelves. Luckily they were out of earshot.

"Sorry!" said the man. "I'm not used to this cloak-and-dagger stuff. Literally, I haven't worn my cloak in years. I've been away . . . "

"Living on a distant island?" asked Kit. "And is your name . . . " She put her fingers to her head, as though working magic. "Ben Picarda?"

"How did you know?" asked the man. He blinked, looking impressed.

"I'm a mighty wizard," said Kit in a mysterious whisper.

"Also, Faith told her," added Josh.

"You're no fun," said Kit.

Ben laughed. "Yes, I'm Ben. And you must be Kit . . . and Alita and Josh?"

"Did the Wizards' Council tell you about us?" asked Alita, nervously playing with one of her thick black braids.

Ben shook his head. "Oh no, I'm too lowly a wizard for them to tell me much. Faith did. She called me on the duradar when she heard I was coming. She said you're both very clever and capable, and I should trust you."

Alita and Josh looked pleased.

"What did she say about me?" asked Kit.

"That you like fireballs, and that you have the potential to be a great wizard, as long as you don't blow yourself up first," said Ben.

Kit was going to object, but then she realized it was a fair summary.

"Welcome to our library," said Alita.

"Apparently we have your mom to thank for its existence?" said Ben.

Alita smiled shyly. "Do you like it?"

"It's magnificent!" he said. "I only got here a couple of minutes ago, so I haven't even had a chance to go downstairs yet to where the real magic happens."

"We can show you the Book Wood if you like?" said Alita, her brown eyes sparkling with excitement.

"Please!" said Ben. "Can't wait to meet the new dragon. I wonder if it's hatched yet. Though, can I confess something? I don't have any experience with real, live dragon care, so I'm a bit nervous."

"That's OK. Alita's really great with dragons," said Kit. "All animals, actually!"

"Excellent!" said Ben. "Lead the way!"

"I'm very good with books!" said Josh, following as Kit and Alita led Ben to the stacks.

"Vitally important!" said Ben, hanging back so Josh wasn't on his own.

As they walked down through the tunnel into the Book Wood, Ben kept stopping to look around him, using the light of a magical flame Kit had conjured. "I haven't actually been in a real library for so long! While I was on the island, I had books but no library. Oh, I've missed this. The smell. The feel of the air. The rustle of the pages . . . "

Kit looked up to see him beaming in the dim light. "Amazing!" he breathed again. "I can just feel the magic tingling!"

"It's nice, isn't it?" said Kit shyly.

Soon they were in the center of the Book Wood. It had grown since yesterday, with the smaller saplings they'd seen then now turned into trees.

"Let's go see if the baby's hatched!" said Alita.

They descended the stairs, chatting as they went.

"What was it like living on an island?" asked Alita. "Were there cool animals?"

"What type of magic were you working on?" asked Josh. "Did you turn into animals?"

"Yes, and I can tell you all about it," said Ben. "But I think it's probably not a good idea to take notes while you're walking down stairs. Call me an ancient killjoy, but that's the way necks get broken."

Josh put away his notebook.

"Later, I promise!" said Ben with a grin. "It's so exciting to be able to share ideas with you. We have so much ahead! Kit, I have so many spells to teach you."

Kit felt her heart swell with possibilities.

All of a sudden, Dogon came barreling through

the air toward them. He landed on Alita's shoulder and started whining.

"Shhh," said Alita. "I'll give you a treat soon."

That didn't stop Dogon. In fact, he only whined louder.

"He really wants that treat!" said Ben, laughing.

Just then, they reached the bottom and entered the dragon's lair, through double doors patterned with tiny scales.

As the light glinted from the mound of treasure in the center of the room, Kit realized that something was wrong.

Very wrong.

The dragon egg was gone.

CHAPTER 8

USES OF A DRAGON EGG

Kit felt her stomach drop. What had happened to the egg? Could someone have taken it? Unless . . . maybe Ben had moved it? But her hopes were dashed as soon as she saw his expression of utter horror.

"Oh, no!" said Ben. He started to pace. "This can't be happening. I should have come down earlier. I shouldn't have waited. This is all my fault. I've failed in the most important part of my job as a wizard. On the first day, I've lost the dragon."

"Don't worry! We'll find it!" said Kit, trying to sound much more confident than she felt.

"Yes," said Josh. "Let's go get Faith!"

That made Ben look even more upset.

"You're probably right," he said, and pulled a glass globe out of his pocket—a duradar. "I'll call her."

When Faith answered the magical phone, Ben told her what had happened. All she said was, "I'm coming. Wait there."

By the time Faith arrived, it was almost time for the children to go to class.

"Kit, Josh, Alita—are you all right?" she asked.

They nodded.

"I'm so sorry," said Ben. He ran his fingers through his hair nervously. They got stuck in a tangle, and he shook his head to free himself. "I can't believe this is happening."

Faith came over and gave him a hug. "You always did tend to lose things. Remember when you managed to lose the cat, back at the Academy? And it turned out to be under your bed, because you forgot you left some fish and chips under there."

That made Ben laugh for a moment. "Oh, yeah. Bosie did like fish and chips."

"Kit, Alita, Josh, go to class. Come back at lunch, and we can see where we've gotten," commanded Faith. "Ben and I will start investigating."

"But I want to help!" said Kit.

"Class!" Faith gave her the Look, and Kit scurried away upstairs.

"Am I . . . going to get fired?" Kit heard Ben whisper as Faith shooed them back up to the school.

"We'll work this out somehow," said Faith. "It's going to be OK."

But as Kit looked back over her shoulder, Ben didn't look OK. He looked like someone who thought it was never going to be OK again.

Classes went painfully slowly before lunch. Even Josh and Alita, who usually loved math, agreed.

"You haven't accidentally done a time-slowing spell, have you?" whispered Josh as Kit copied his answers.

"I wish I could do that," said Kit. "But no. If I could, I'd be doing a fast-forward spell right now!"

After what felt like nine hours, the lunch bell rang. Alita and Josh rushed to the library while

Kit grabbed her lunch. This was an emergency, but there was no way she was dealing with an emergency on an empty stomach. After gulping down her three sandwiches, she joined them all down in the Book Wood.

A desk was now set up in the forest, surrounded by chairs that looked like they'd been taken from the school storage room. On the table were piles of books.

"Sorry it's not much," said Ben. "I was going to make a real common room when the Book Wood had grown more. But, without the dragon . . . " He trailed off, looking ashamed.

"It's plenty for now," said Faith. "Kit, we were starting to do some research to see who or what might have taken the egg. You three can take over. Ben and I will go do some investigating out in the world."

"Why can't I do investigating out in the world?" asked Kit, looking in despair at the huge pile of books.

"Because it's a school day, and you have to be

back to class in forty-five minutes!" said Faith. "But we'll see you after school, down here, right?"

Josh and Alita, already deep into books, didn't answer. Kit nodded.

"Are you sure we can't let them skip school this once?" asked Ben.

Faith gave him a Look.

"Point taken," said Ben. "Happy researching! We'll see you later!"

Kit picked up a book on dragon eggs. Alita had one about dark magic spells, and Josh was deep in a volume called *Uses of Magical Eggs of Diverse Kinds*.

Kit's own book didn't make for fun reading. She read about monsters that ate dragon eggs, and about a time when a dragon egg cracked and blew up a building. *I can't believe this book is making me hate reading about explosions,* she thought glumly. Normally, when it came to joyful reading experiences, explosions were up there with car chases and people falling in poop as far as Kit was concerned.

Josh, meanwhile, was furiously taking notes. Kit peered over his shoulder.

Apparently one evil wizard collected dragon eggs in the past, stopped them from hatching using a spell, and hoarded them so he could use their power one day if he needed to. Like how my cousin keeps all his action figures in their boxes and won't play with them. But evil.

Suddenly Alita gasped and looked up from her book. "Oh, no! I just read that with a particular spell, you could use the power of a dragon egg to basically wipe out life on earth. The eggs are even more powerful for some spells than living dragons!"

"Well, that's incredibly terrifying," said Josh.

"Maybe it's just a weird collector like in Josh's book," said Kit quickly.

There was a buzzing sound—the school bell. Alita and Josh started packing up. "We could just stay down here," said Kit. "Faith and Ben would never know."

But there was another buzzing sound. This time

it came from Kit's pocket. She reached inside and pulled out something she hadn't noticed was in there. A small square of what looked like paper. It was vibrating. The paper said: *Get to class. This paper will keep buzzing in a really annoying way until you do. Love, Faith.*

Kit sighed and put the paper back in her pocket. "That was sneaky of her," she said, but she headed up toward school anyway. Apparently there was no escaping the watchful eye of Faith.

CHAPTER 9

CEMETERY

After school, Kit, Alita, Josh, Ben, and Faith gathered in the Book Wood underneath the public library, down in the common room, which sat nestled in a tree. It was very cozy with its battered armchairs, and Faith had brought some ginger cake for them to eat as they plotted.

"I've been asking around," said Faith. "A wizard I know saw some hooded figures in the cemetery, near the abandoned church. He walks his dog that way, and he thought he overheard something that might be a spell. I went to check, and there was no one there, but my thaumometer showed traces of past spells that mean someone's been doing a lot of magic there. Dark magic," she added. "What did you find, Ben?"

"Nothing so far," said Ben glumly. "Maybe we should all do some more research?"

"I think we should all go check out the cemetery," said Kit.

"You just don't want to do any more research," accused Josh.

"No, I don't just not want to do any more research. I don't want to do any more research *and* I think we should check out the cemetery. They might come back! Or we might find clues!"

"Maybe it's worth a try," said Faith. "Everyone could use some air. And you might spot something I missed."

"I think we should stay at the cemetery until they come back!" suggested Kit.

"So, like, a stakeout?" asked Josh. He'd been sneakily reading a detective novel in art class. "We should have a thermos of coffee if it is. I don't like coffee, but I don't make the rules of detective novels."

Faith brought out a thermos. "No coffee, but here's some chocolate tea. I think we can bend the rules to have something we actually want to drink."

Josh took it eagerly.

At the cemetery, they headed for the abandoned church and settled down to wait.

And wait.

And wait.

No one turned up except a couple of joggers.

"Unless that man's doing a spell to make his face as red as a tomato, I don't think he's a wizard," said Josh, disappointed.

"While we wait, tell us what you found out during your lunchtime research," said Ben.

"I found out that Faith bugged my pocket with a magic piece of paper," said Kit.

Faith smiled. "My motto is *trust, but also verify*."

"We also found out that some monsters eat dragon eggs. So maybe there's a monster in the school?" asked Kit.

"All the monsters I've met so far have been nice," said Alita. "Lizzy was lovely!"

"Those mermaids weren't very nice. Or the Dragon Masters," said Josh. "Although I don't know if mermaids are monsters, technically."

"Monster isn't a technical term," said Alita, playing with her braids thoughtfully. "It's just a thing humans call creatures they don't like."

"Very true," said Ben. "After all, some people call dragons monsters, and"—he made a sweeping gesture—"well, you know the truth about dragons. Dragons are amazing and wonderful—"

"It's not a monster, I don't think," said Faith, interrupting Ben, who looked like he was going to go off on a long speech about the amazingness of dragons. "I searched the Book Wood and the rest of the school, and there were no traces of wild magic that didn't come from the dragon egg itself. We're pretty sure it must have been a human wizard. Or wizards . . . "

She trailed off, looking around at the trees and the graves nearby. "Kit, Ben, did you feel something?"

Ben shook his head. "Kit, can you?"

Kit focused her mind. "There's . . . something. I can't quite tell. It's like something's blocking me. Like I can't see clearly . . . "

"It's a spell, isn't it?" said Josh. He glanced around. "Where's the wizard?"

Faith pulled out her thaumometer, holding it up to the air. "I have this programmed to recognize my, Kit's, and Ben's magic, so it will be able to spot any other spellwork nearby."

She waved it around. The closer she pointed it to the empty chapel, the more it glowed. Faith frowned. "Hmm, I'm getting very confused readings. The thaumometer thinks there's a spell being cast right in front of us!"

They all turned to stare at the empty chapel, then back at the glowing thaumometer.

"There isn't anyone there," Josh whispered.

"Let me try mine," said Ben. He pulled out another thaumometer, which was like Faith's but had an extra gem. "I made some modifications while I was on the island, to detect more distant magic. I have a theory . . . " He held up the device in the air, and a moment later both gems glowed, then flashed. "Oh!" said Ben. He turned to Faith and Kit. "It's an echo. The magic isn't actually here! It's in another part of the cemetery, and there's a spell bouncing it here to put us off the scent."

"Sneaky," said Faith. "They're cleverer than I thought. And therefore, more dangerous. I think it's best if Ben and I go and check this out on our own," she said. "You three should go home. It's too risky. We might need to use battle magic."

"We'll be fine!" said Kit.

"Yes," said Faith. "Because you're going home."

She gave them one of her Looks.

"I think we should go home," said Josh with a grimace. "She's doing the Look."

Faith nodded in approval. "Come on, Ben," she said.

The two adult wizards walked off down the path, Ben's thaumometer held out in front of them.

"Go home!" called Faith without looking back.

The children started walking toward the exit.

"Are we really going home?" asked Josh.

"Of course not," said Kit. "They're out of sight now. Let's turn around."

Alita was looking at her closely. "You've got a weird look on your face. What is it, Kit?"

Kit tried to put it into words. "There's something here, in the air. It feels . . . like someone's doing some pretty intense magic."

It was like the feeling she got close to a dragon, crossed with the feeling she'd had when they'd defeated the Dragon Masters. Big magic. Old magic.

"Where?" asked Alita, watching her closely.

"I think it's nearby. Despite what Ben's thaumometer said. There's something here." She shivered. Whatever the spell was, it was making the little hairs on the back of her neck stand at attention.

"Maybe we should go home," said Alita. "Faith told us to."

"You can," said Kit. "I'm staying."

Alita sighed. "No. We stay together or we all go."

"How about we stay, but run away really fast if something bad happens?" Josh suggested.

They made their way back through the graveyard, down a leafy alley. The feeling inside Kit grew stronger. "There's dark magic here somewhere." They were beside the chapel now. The air was humming with magic. It made Kit's stomach feel queasy. This magic felt wrong, like someone was reaching inside her and twisting something. "I can feel it . . . but I can't see anything."

"Well," said Alita, "that doesn't mean there isn't anything, does it? Evil wizards aren't going to play fair. So maybe they've hidden themselves somehow."

"Invisible evil wizards!" said Josh. "Of course! Illusion magic! I know a counterspell you can use. It makes hidden things visible."

"Teach me?" said Kit.

"Faith's already taught you it," Josh said, frowning.

"Uh, I forgot it," said Kit with a blush. Keeping all the spells she'd been taught in her head was a battle. She wished she had more room in there! It was such a crowded jumble.

Josh sighed. "You raise your hands, palms forward. Yes, like that. Then repeat the spell after me."

Break the light into atoms
The dark inside dehors
Take this eye to the truth.

Kit repeated the spell, holding her palms out. The air began to shimmer and shake, like a bubble stretching and popping.

Then, all of a sudden, the chapel wasn't empty. Through the window, they saw a group of hooded figures standing in a circle, chanting.

In the center of the circle was a shape.

The egg.

One of the robed figures turned: a young man with bright blond hair.

"We have company," he said. He raised an arm, and light shot out from his fingertips. Toward Alita.

CHAPTER 10

THE RESCUE

Alita crumpled to the ground with a gasp.

"No!" cried Kit. She rushed forward, hands raised, frantically running through spells in her mind. Which to use? Which to use? She felt panic rising. The robed man was raising his hands to hurl another spell at her.

"Shield spell!" hissed Josh.

She remembered.

"*Tortuga!*" she cried, crisscrossing her hands to create an invisible shield—just in time, as a fireball hurtled toward them. The shield absorbed the hit

but shivered and shook. Kit looked down at Alita. Josh was kneeling beside her.

"Is she OK?"

Alita groaned in reply.

Kit shuddered as another fireball hit the shield.

"It's just kids," the blond man called to the other hooded wizards. "Keep going, I've got this covered!" His hands crackled with energy. It might be something more powerful than a fireball this time.

Kit was going to have to counterattack. She sent more energy into the shield spell, letting it flow through her fingers, then prepared to hurl a fireball of her own at the blond man.

The chanting of the hooded wizards grew louder. They were raising their hands. She let the energy build within her, and cast the fireball spell toward her enemy.

The blond man cried out a shield spell just as her fireball hit, but it made him stagger.

"Hit him again!" said Josh.

Kit glanced at Alita, who still looked wobbly, the warmth in her brown skin drained. Kit felt a stab of guilt. She'd made her stay. She'd gotten Alita hurt.

Kit cast another fireball spell, but she knew she wasn't focusing as well as she should. The small fireball dissolved against the evil wizard's shield with a pathetic *pffft*.

"Child, you can't break my shield. You can't stop this," snarled the blond man. Then he turned to the robed figures and cried, "Keep going!"

They answered by raising their voices as they chanted. Magic built in the air around them. There was a mighty cracking sound, and a blast of light flowed into each of the figures, including the blond man.

Kit didn't know what to do. If she sent a fireball at them now that the blond man wasn't fighting back, she might hurt the egg.

There was a crack in the undergrowth behind them. Kit's heart thumped in terror. *There are more of them!* she thought. *They've got us.*

But as branches parted, she saw Ben and Faith. Faith put a finger to her lips. Then she and Ben raised their hands and cried out.

"Telay parrah, away to far!"

Faith swiped her flat hand through the air, and Ben mirrored the gesture. Energy began to build between them.

"What?" cried the blond man, turning from his spell to see Faith and Ben emerging from the bushes. "NO!"

Just then, Faith and Ben flung their arms out in front of them, releasing the energy from their spell.

The blond man released a counterspell as the energy engulfed him and his robed followers. Kit saw it coming for them. For Josh. It was headed right toward him. She couldn't find words for a spell of her own. Time seemed to slow.

Then everything happened quicker than light. There was a thunderclap, and a cloud of shadows snatched the robed figures away into thin air.

With a yell of *"Theostru!"* Faith snuffed out the evil wizard's spell before it hit Josh.

"Oh," said Josh. He staggered slightly, then steadied himself. "Well, that was close."

"What happened? Where did they go?" asked Kit.

Sweet-smelling smoke rose all around the chapel, and they could barely make out the ruined stones.

"We teleported them away," said Ben. "I don't know if they'll be back, but we should be safe for now. But I fear whatever spell they were casting, they managed to finish." He waved at the smoke. "That's not from our teleportation spell."

"Are you OK?" asked Faith. The cemetery was quiet. All Kit could hear was the thumping of blood in her ears.

"We're OK, but Alita was hit," said Kit with another stab of guilt.

"With what?" asked Faith.

"Some kind of energy-bolt spell. She hit her head," said Josh.

"'M OK," muttered Alita.

"I'll be the judge of that," said Faith. "Look at me, Alita," she said, passing her fingers back and forth before Alita's eyes. "Follow my finger."

"What spell are you doing?" asked Josh, getting out his notebook.

"First aid," said Faith. "Part of every wizard librarian's training."

Josh looked a bit disappointed.

Faith got Alita to walk in a straight line, then stand on one leg. Finally she was satisfied. "No concussion, but you should take it easy for a while," she said.

Turning to Kit, Faith said, "We can talk later about why you didn't go home like you were told. First, I think we need to check out the chapel."

As they headed into the ruined church, the smoke began to clear and they could see where the wizards had been circled around the egg.

The egg was gone. But as they got closer, Kit saw something on the ground.

Something . . . moving.

If she wasn't mistaken, it was a baby dragon.

CHAPTER 11

BABY BLUE

A cracked shell lay on the ground, and the dragon—a just-waking, tiny dragon—was blinking up at them. It was blue, with bright-purple eyes.

"A blue!" Ben gasped. "The rarest kind of dragon!"

"It's beautiful!" said Alita.

"I think we stopped them just in time!" said Ben. He leaned against a pillar, looking very pale. "Phew. That was intense. I . . . don't remember that teleportation spell being so tiring."

Kit, Alita, and Josh gathered around the dragon.

"Are you OK?" asked Alita, reaching out to stroke

it, then stopping. "Is it OK to touch it? I won't hurt it, will I?"

"It's fine," said Faith. "Let the little one sniff your finger so it knows your scent first."

Alita did so, and the dragon gave her a great big lick with its forked tongue.

Kit was feeling too worried to get any closer herself. She kept glancing at Alita. She still looked pale. Was she OK?

Why did I let them stay with me? I should have done it on my own.

"Aww, it's so cute!" Alita giggled as the dragon licked her hand.

Then Kit had a thought. "Wait . . . isn't an awake dragon bad? Isn't that what caused the Great Fire of London?" She listened, in case a rumbling was coming that signified bad things. But all was quiet in the graveyard.

Faith laughed. "I think we're OK," she said.

"They're meant to be awake for the first month of life," said Josh. "In one of the egg-care books I read, it says they only go to sleep when they're ready." He looked down at the dragon. "That one doesn't look very happy, though."

"Do you think it's male or female?" asked Alita.

"There's no way of telling unless you ask it," said Faith. "We'll have to wait until it's asleep to ask. Dragons can't talk when they're awake."

The dragon coughed, letting out a little puff of smoke. "Is that normal?" asked Kit.

"Perfectly normal. Baby dragons tend to build up some fire in their lungs before they hatch. It's just letting it out," said Faith. "But I bet being egg-napped was a shock."

"Are you OK, little one?" asked Ben, leaning down and holding out his hand for the dragon to sniff. The baby dragon licked his hand and then nuzzled into him, letting out the saddest noise, like a lamb that's just realized it's lost its mother.

"Oh!" said Alita, hand on her heart. "The poor thing! How can we help?"

"We can take it home," said Faith. "Then we can find out who those wizards were. And I can think of the right punishment for you three for disobeying me."

The children groaned. Although, Kit realized, she didn't mind being punished. She just wanted Alita and Josh to be safe. And she decided she wasn't going to let anything like that happen again, ever. She was a wizard, and her friends weren't. She couldn't let them take the same risks as she did.

They made their way slowly back to Chatsworth Library and through the tunnels to the Book Wood beneath the school. Josh was scribbling notes in his book, while Kit, Faith, and Alita carried the shards of the dragon's egg very carefully, and Ben carried the dragon. It seemed to like him, and was asleep in his arms within minutes.

"Wait, is the dragon going to sleep for real? Already?" asked Josh.

"No, this is a normal sleep, like any baby creature that's had a tiring few hours," said Faith.

Ben looked down at the sleepy dragon in his arms. They were nearly at the school's Book Wood and the little one was stirring. "This one deserves to be read to a lot to get over the shock."

They took the dragon carefully down to its lair and laid it to rest on its hoard. After Alita adjusted its tail to make sure it was comfortable, Faith and Ben cast extra protection spells over the dragon, and Faith taught Kit a new one to use on the door to the lair.

"Still, we should stay to guard it," said Faith. "I'll take first watch. Kit, Alita, Josh, your punishment for disobeying me is . . . chewing-gum duty."

"Ewww!" said the three children in unison. But they headed back up to the library and got started.

Once they'd scraped sticky disgusting wads of gum off the undersides of all the library tables, Ben looked at his watch. "Right," he said. "You've got about . . . fifteen minutes to do all your homework before the library closes. Go! I have some shelving to do."

He wandered off, and the children sat down in a quiet corner and got their notebooks out.

"Can I copy yours?" Kit asked Alita.

"I haven't done it yet," said Alita. "You've been with me the whole time!"

"Can I copy yours?" Kit asked Josh.

Josh paused.

"You've already done it, haven't you?" said Kit.

"When?" asked Alita.

"When we were walking back through the tunnels," said Josh. "I finished writing about the wizards in the graveyard so I thought I'd do my homework."

Kit took the notebook from him. "I thought this was just for magic stuff."

"Homework *is* magic, if you do it right," said Josh.

Kit rolled her eyes, but that didn't mean she wasn't going to copy Josh's work.

CHAPTER 12

A TREE OF GO-KARTS

I've been thinking," said Josh on the school playground the next morning. "Why did those wizards steal the egg?"

"Does it matter?" asked Kit. "We got the dragon back!"

"Yes, it does, actually," said Josh. "If there are a bunch of people out there stealing dragon eggs, we should stop them. We're the good guys—it's our job. And what if they try to steal the dragon again?"

"Didn't Ben and Faith just say we shouldn't be going after evil wizards?" asked Alita. "Not that I'm scared of evil wizards. But I am scared of getting into trouble."

"Actually, you make a good point," said Josh. "I'm scared, too. But we wouldn't get into trouble just for researching them, would we?"

"Do you think Ben has any books on evil wizards in the school library?" asked Kit.

"Let's find out!" said Alita, eyes glinting. "A book hunt!"

Kit pretended to yawn, but she had to admit she was a *bit* interested in finding out why a bunch of evil wizards might want to steal a dragon egg . . . and if that meant reading more, she would just have to be brave and face the music. Or rather, the pages.

When they arrived at the library, Ben was already there, tidying up some books.

"Can we go down to the stacks and find some books on evil wizards?" asked Josh.

Ben chuckled. "Well, hello to you, too."

"Sorry. Hello, Mr. Picarda," said Alita.

"Call me Ben," said Ben. "Mr. Picarda is just for

when other students are listening. And please, go on down. I'm on guard duty with the baby dragon, and I've got some protections set up, but you won't trip them. And I've started stocking the stacks a little more, so you'll find a whole section on dark magic toward the end of the corridor where the Book Wood begins. Mind you, dark magic is a matter of perspective. I'm not sure I agree with calling magic *dark*. It's all about your intention. A so-called dark spell could do good in the right hands."

"Are my hands the right hands?" asked Kit. She looked at her palms. They were already covered in ink stains, and something that looked like oatmeal, from her breakfast.

"Absolutely!" Ben grinned.

Josh was scribbling notes.

Not all dark magic is evil. It's only evil if you use it that way. Mr. Picarda is so cool. Look at his hair!

"Let's go research," said Alita, tugging on Josh's sleeve. "We only have twenty minutes before school starts!"

"Sorry, I haven't made the common room in the Book Wood yet," said Ben. "I'll do that later today. But there's still the table to sit at down there."

Down in the tunnels, they found a collection of books on a shelf labeled "So-Called Dark Magic" and took a few to read. They sat down at Ben's table in the forest.

"This one says baby dragons can be used in wish-granting magic, if you trap them in magical bonds and siphon their magic off over years. I wonder if that's what they were planning!" said Josh.

That idea was too much for Alita, and she had to go and check on the dragon while Kit and Josh carried on reading. They couldn't find any spells that contained the words they'd heard in the cemetery, but they did find a lot more books on uses of dragons' eggs and baby dragons.

Kit found one that said baby dragons could be used to create other magical creatures. *Like Dogon!* she thought. "I wonder if they were going to breed their own race of, like, battle creatures using the baby dragon's magic. That would be awesome!" She pictured having her own tiger-dragon to ride into battle.

"That would be very bad," said Josh disapprovingly.

"Things can be bad *and* awesome at the same time," objected Kit.

"It's a good thing I'm here to be your conscience," Josh said with a sniff. "Otherwise I worry you could become an evil wizard!"

"Never!" said Kit. "I'm one of the good guys! You said!"

"Well, good guys don't turn baby dragons into battle tigers," said Josh.

"OK, fine," said Kit. "I was only saying." Josh took everything so literally. Though, on the plus side, he had taught her what the word *literally* meant.

In all the breaks between lessons, they continued researching spells that might require a stolen baby dragon. Faith joined them sometimes, leaving Greg, the assistant librarian, in charge of Draca and the Chatsworth Library, and bringing books of her own to help.

"The spell we overheard . . . " she said, flipping pages as they sat in the Book Wood beneath the school. "I haven't been able to find it anywhere. I fear it isn't in any book—that it's a new spell, crafted by those wizards. I think we missed too much of it to be able to piece it together."

Kit was getting annoyed. "Why are we bothering with research, then, if we can't find out what the spell was?"

"Because we might be able to think our way around the problem. And because those wizards are still out there. Who knows what they're up to now?" said Faith.

"Maybe we should take a break, though," suggested Ben. "I have a few spells Kit might like to try." He leaned over and whispered in Faith's ear.

She laughed. "Well, sure, you can teach her that. You've got too much hair, anyway."

And so, over the next few days, Ben taught Kit how to breathe fire. It wasn't a very useful spell, but it was a *lot* of fun. Kit only burned Ben's hair off once, and he was able to do a spell to replace it right away. Then he taught her a spell that extinguished other spells—and fires—quickly.

In between spells and research—and the annoying interruptions to magic that were ordinary school classes—Kit and the others visited the new baby dragon and wandered in the growing Book Wood.

"It's not growing quite as quickly as it should," Ben apologized as he and Kit walked there one break, while Josh and Alita were at math club. "Because the dragon hatched outside the library, we lost that magical energy that would have made the trees grow faster. But if you help me plant some books with some growing spells, we should be able to make it all catch up in a couple of weeks."

Kit felt worried about that. She'd had a houseplant once and accidentally killed it because she tried to feed it perfume to make it smell nice. But Ben said the Book Wood trees were tough.

"They're full of ideas," he said. "And ideas can survive a lot."

So they planted books and said spells over them.

"These spells combine with the magic of the dragon," Ben explained. "Look."

As the spell worked, one of the books they'd planted shot up into a sapling, with crinkly bark and unfurling green leaves, written all over in black ink.

Kit shivered, feeling the magic go through her. It wasn't a bad shiver. It was like the feeling Kit had when she listened to a piece of music that made her want to cry, but because it was beautiful, not because she was sad.

"It's lovely, isn't it?" said Ben. "It must be hard for your friends, not having the powers you have."

Kit shrugged. "They've got other powers. Like math."

"Wouldn't it be great if magic was for everyone, though?" said Ben. "If everyone could benefit from what we have?"

Kit had never thought about that. "What, if everyone in the world was a wizard?"

"No, I mean if we could help everyone with magic," said Ben. "If the Wizards' Council wasn't in charge of all magic. If we could do what we wanted with it. If we could . . . I don't know, cure cancer. Cast a spell to stop people from hurting other people! Or just make everyone's lives a little better."

Kit was shocked hearing a grown-up talk like that. But she liked it.

"Faith said the Wizards' Council thinks magic shouldn't be used to solve human problems," said Kit. "People have tried in the past and it's gone badly."

Ben shrugged. "Personally I think they shouldn't judge everyone so harshly."

"People *do* use magic for bad things, though. Like stealing dragon eggs!" pointed out Kit. Although she was starting to think he did have a point.

"There have always been evil wizards," said Ben. "That doesn't mean all wizards are evil." He shrugged again. "Sorry, I'm just thinking out loud. I do a lot of that. Been on an island on my own for too long, I suppose!" He laughed. "Come on. Let's go and get the others. I've got something to show you all."

Kit went to fetch Alita and Josh, and they wandered through the Book Wood until they reached a tree with a door in it.

"I finally got around to it! We have a common room!" said Ben. His face lit up as he opened the doors to the tree and ushered them inside. When they reached the top, it was very different to the common room in Faith's library.

"I got a bit carried away, sorry," said Ben, blushing.

The common room was huge, with an area of squishy armchairs and tables and books . . . but there was also a go-kart track! Each of the karts was designed to look like a dragon.

"Whoa!" said Kit, jumping into one of them, looking for a way to start it.

"You have to use magic," said Ben. "Watch."

He brushed his hand across the steering wheel and said, *"Allezee!"*

The go-kart lurched into motion and Kit zoomed off, whooping.

"The spell to stop it is '*arrett!*' and stroke the wheel the other way!" Ben yelled after her. But Kit was in no hurry to stop. She zoomed around the track, still whooping.

The others crept up to the track, more hesitant.

"Hop in," Kit heard Ben call over the sound of her kart.

Alita and Josh climbed into karts of their own, and Ben said the spell to make them both start. Soon they were following Kit around the track.

"This is awesome!" said Josh. "I'm going to die, I think, but it's still awesome!"

"You're not going to die!" yelled Kit. "WHOOOOOO!"

Alita wasn't saying anything. She was just squealing like a guinea pig who's eaten too much sugar. Kit couldn't tell if she was scared or having the time of her life, or both.

"*Arrett!*" Ben cried.

Their karts came to a halt, all pointing toward him. He was holding a duradar and looking grim.

"Sorry to end the fun," he said. "But I just got a call from Faith. Something has happened. Something very, very bad."

CHAPTER 13

SOMETHING NASTY IN THE CHAPEL

As they rushed through the tunnels to the public library, all Ben could tell them was that Greg had arrived at the library with bad news and that Faith was trying to get the full story out of him. Greg didn't make much sense at the best of times, and this was clearly far from the best of times. All he'd said, over and over, was, "There's something nasty in the chapel. Something nasty in the chapel."

Greg and Faith were waiting for them in the common room. Faith glanced up with worried eyes. "Hi," she said.

Greg was drinking tea and eating cookies. His hand was shaking a little. Faith was sitting next to him, feeding him extra cookies and talking to him in a low, soothing voice. The children gathered around.

"What happened?" asked Kit.

Greg looked up, but his eyes seemed to look through her. "*Whoosh! Kaboom!* They're in the chapel. They appeared. They weren't there. Then they were there," he said, which didn't clear anything up.

"I think we need to use a spell to help him," said Faith. "But carefully. Mind magic is dangerous."

"*Kaboom!*" agreed Greg. "Can I have a cookie?"

Ben passed him a chocolate cookie and Greg crunched down on it, getting crumbs in his long white beard.

"There's something nasty in the chapel," he added as soon as his mouth wasn't too full.

"Greg, can we use a spell to help you remember exactly what happened?" Faith asked. Her voice was low and steady but her eyes were full of fear.

Greg nodded. "It's all a great mass of tails and

teeth," he said. "They're here. They're here. There's something nasty in the chapel."

"Ben, would you pass me the circlet? It's on the top shelf."

Ben went and fetched something that looked like a crown made from twirling, twisting silver, and Faith placed it gently on Greg's head.

Faith kept her hands on the crown and began to chant.

Take me to the mind
Take the mind from the noise
Tooshay tooshay the heart of the vision
Sight return from noise, truth from cloud
Take me to the mind.

All sound was sucked from the room, except for the sound of breathing. Kit couldn't tell whose breath she could hear, but it was hard and fast. They were scared. Everything went dark for a moment, and then was replaced with the sight of green leaves twisted around graves. Tree roots were tripping her as she stumbled closer to something. She could smell fresh earth and grass and damp leaves. Her heart felt like it would burst with fear.

It was Greg's heart. She didn't know how she knew, but she knew.

Her bones felt old. Everything creaked and ached. She reached out to pull a branch aside to get a better look.

The scene beyond the trees came into closer focus. A clearing. A tall, ruined building.

"We're in the cemetery," said Faith. Kit couldn't see her, but she felt that she was somewhere close by.

"What's Greg looking at?" asked Kit.

"I don't know yet. I can see figures moving, but they're blurred," said Faith.

Then Kit could see them, too. They became clearer and clearer, until she saw that they were a group of men, all in hooded robes. One had blond hair.

"I've seen him!" said Kit. "It's the man from before, the one who had the dragon egg!"

"Yes," said Faith. "But what are they standing around? I can see shapes inside the circle. Large shapes."

There were creatures in the center of the circle, on all fours. They were covered in ragged fur and their eyes glowed red.

Rats. They were rats. Giant ones.

Then they rose, stretching up to the height of the men, their beady red eyes blazing.

The blond man began to speak. "We did it! We brought them back! Go, tell him to come."

"The hatching energy did its job," said one of the robed figures. "It gave them the strength to break through. Now all we need is a day for them to regain their full strength."

"Faith," whispered Kit. "Are they . . . Did they bring them back?"

"It looks like it," said Faith. "They never wanted the baby dragon. They just wanted to use the power of the hatching egg."

"The Dragon Masters," said Kit.

The rats in the center of the circle staggered as they walked, and the blond man gestured to them, passing some kind of energy across them.

"Someone's here," said another of the men. "In the bushes."

The blond man held up a hand. "He mustn't see!"

A wave of force threw Kit off her wobbly feet.

Off Greg's feet.

Then she vanished, and she was back in the library, panting.

"What happened?" asked Alita.

"What did you see?" asked Josh.

"The Dragon Masters," said Kit. "Didn't we, Faith?"

Faith didn't reply. Kit turned to see that she was still standing with her hands touching the crown on Greg's head, still in the vision.

"Faith?" said Ben. "Faith, are you OK?"

Faith and Greg both let out a gasp. Then Faith fell to the floor, and Greg slumped to one side.

"Faith!" yelled Kit.

Ben bounded to her side, while Alita and Josh went to Greg.

"Faith, wake up!" said Ben. He sounded desperate.

"Greg! Greg!" said Alita. "Wake up!"

"What's wrong with them?" asked Kit. "What's happening?"

Ben looked at her with hollow eyes. "The spell . . . it went wrong. They're in a trance, and I don't know how to wake them." He made an anguished face. "I should have volunteered to do it. Mind magic is dangerous. She said so, and I still let her do it."

"No one *lets* Faith do anything," murmured Josh.

"Here, help me get her into a chair," said Ben. Kit and Josh helped lift Faith into an armchair. She felt as heavy as lead, but still warm. With a lot of puffing and panting on Kit's and Josh's parts, she was in a chair next to Greg. Side by side they both looked like they were just staring into space. But Kit felt an unnatural glimmer of magic in the air. This wasn't a normal sleep.

"We should call an ambulance," said Alita.

"It won't do any good," said Ben. "They're not ill. This is a magical trance, from the spell. I think . . . because Greg was in such a state, he sucked Faith's mind down with his. I'm afraid if we try to cure them with a spell, we could cause more harm."

"What can we do, then?" asked Josh. "Is there a book?" He sounded doubtful. That scared Kit. Josh thinking a book couldn't fix something meant you were facing a truly terrible problem.

Ben shook his head. "I think it's time for me to go see the Wizards' Council." He swallowed hard, making his Adam's apple bob up and down like he'd swallowed a golf ball. "I'll go and ask them to fix this. And tell them it's my fault. I lost the dragon, then I allowed this to happen."

Kit felt a pang of sadness, followed by the stirring of determination. "No!" she said. "We can solve this ourselves. We don't need to go running to the council. We're not babies."

"But we're not all-powerful ancient wizards in possession of the wisdom of the centuries, either," pointed out Josh.

"No, but we fought Salt on our own, didn't we? We defeated the ancient ghost rats from the dawn of time, and the mind-controlled mermaids."

"But now those rats are back," said Ben. "And they're not ghosts anymore. Kit, this is beyond us. I know you're a powerful wizard, and you're very capable. But I need to bring in the big guns now." He looked at her very seriously. "Don't do anything until I get back, OK? I couldn't bear it if you got hurt."

Kit nodded. The other children did, too.

"I'll get Dogon to watch over Faith and Greg when we go home," said Alita. "And we can check on them in the morning."

"Good," said Ben. "They won't need to eat or drink, at least, in this kind of mystical coma. Cheer up, Kit. They might just wake up on their own. And if not, the council will know how to fix it."

Kit sighed deeply. She couldn't believe there was nothing she could do.

"Now go and get some rest," said Ben. "You all must be exhausted. And, Kit, I'll get this fixed, I promise. My mess, my cleanup."

"But I don't want the council to punish you. This isn't all your fault!" said Kit.

"It doesn't matter whose fault it is in the end," said Ben. "We just need help. OK? Don't do anything till I get back. Promise?"

"OK," said Kit, crossing her fingers behind her back.

There was no way she was waiting for Ben. She was going to fix this, and make sure the Wizards' Council had nothing to punish him for.

CHAPTER 14

THE TOMB

The children were all at Alita's house for dinner, and after more helpings of food than even Kit really wanted, they retreated to Alita's bedroom.

"Tell me everything you saw," said Josh, notebook out.

Kit described every moment of the vision, including the part at the end where the blond man cast a spell on Greg to scramble his mind. "And that's when the vision ended," she finished.

"I can't believe the Dragon Masters are back," said Alita. She bit her lip and turned her eyes to the ground. "I thought we beat them, you know? I thought we won last time."

"They did say they'd return," said Kit.

"All villains say they'll be back," said Josh. "It's just what villains do."

"But apparently these ones keep their promises," said Alita. "Which is really annoying. Villains are supposed to break promises, not keep them."

"Speaking of breaking promises," said Kit, "I don't want to just sit here and wait for Ben. I want to do something."

She waited for her friends to yell at her, but instead they both nodded.

"We can't just leave Ben to do this. This isn't like disobeying Faith when she told you not to go after Salt. Ben's our friend, and we can't let the council punish him for something that's actually the fault of evil wizards," said Alita.

"Plus, the Wizards' Council takes *so* long to make up their minds. This might be all over before they decide what to do," said Josh. "Sometimes the fact that you're rash and hasty is useful."

Kit grinned with relief. "Oh, good. I thought I was going to have to be rash and hasty on my own." She felt a pang of worry, though. Should she really be bringing the others with her on dangerous missions? After what happened to Alita? After what could have happened?

"You definitely shouldn't do things on your own," said Josh. "We're a team. Even if we're a very, very scared team," he added.

"OK, then. In the morning, we begin," said Kit.

The next morning they went to check on Faith and Greg. They were exactly the same—staring into space, seeing nothing, as though they were frozen in time. Josh brewed up some chocolate tea with ingredients he'd brought from home, and they wafted their cups under Faith's nose before drinking it themselves.

"I hope Ben's not getting shouted at too much by the Wizards' Council," said Kit. She'd been on the receiving end of Branwen's sarcasm, and that was when she wasn't even angry.

"One thing that's been bothering me, though,"

said Alita, "is why the Dragon Masters didn't appear right away, when the evil wizards did their spell over the egg."

"Oh, I know," said Josh. "I read about some spells that don't happen right after you finish saying them. Some really big spells take time to brew. Like tea."

"Evil tea," said Kit. "And not even the chocolate kind."

"I've written up what we know so far, so we know where to start," said Josh. He got out his notebook and showed them.

What we know: evil wizards have brought back the Dragon Masters using a spell and energy from

the hatching of the dragon's egg. Greg saw them in the cemetery, and they did something to scramble his brain. Then when Faith tried to help unscramble it, she got sucked into Greg's vision, and she's now in a mystical coma, which is like a normal coma but with magic and no beeping machines.

What we don't know: whether there's any link between what's happening now and what happened when the cursed bone nearly brought back the Dragon Masters over the summer.

POOR GREG

What we need to find out: how to get Faith and Greg out of their mystical comas and stop the Dragon Masters and their evil wizard friends before the Wizards' Council punishes Ben and he has to live as an exile all alone and sad, which he doesn't deserve because he is cool and nice.

"Anyway," said Josh. "I've got an idea. I've been reading this detective book where, when they want to find out what happened, they go back to the scene of the crime. So if we go back to where Greg's mind got messed with, and where the Dragon Masters were, we might find something that'll help."

"What if the Dragon Masters are still there?" asked Alita.

"Then we run away," said Josh. "Really, really fast. And think of a new plan."

When they reached the cemetery, it was deserted. Not a rat or an evil wizard in sight. It was a gray day, and a little chilly under the trees. Kit was glad she had a stomach full of chocolate tea and snacks to warm her up. Alita had a woolly sweater on over her dress, and Josh was wearing his long raincoat. "Just in case," he said. "Also, it makes me look like a detective."

They walked all around the chapel, where they'd seen the Dragon Masters and the evil wizards in Greg's vision. At first, they found nothing. But when they walked around again, looking more carefully at the ground, Josh found a clue.

It was a shred of cloak, hanging off the stone door to a tomb. The door to the tomb was ajar.

"That's the same color cloak as that blond wizard was wearing," said Josh. "A clue!"

Kit came closer and peered at it. She was starting to get a nasty feeling about all this.

"There!" said Alita. "Look at those marks in the mud. It's like someone's opened that door recently."

"You don't think it's vampires, do you?" asked Josh, looking around nervously.

"It's daylight," said Kit. "And vampires don't exist."

"In which case," said Josh, "I don't want to jump to conclusions. But I have a serious worry that the entrance to the evil wizards' lair is in that tomb."

"I think you're right," said Kit.

"So we have to go in to investigate, don't we?" said Josh, not moving. "If my grandma ever finds out I climbed inside a tomb, I am so dead," he added. "We're practically grave-robbing. She'll *kill* me."

"I'll cry a lot at your funeral," said Alita. "And wear a very nice black hat. Now, let's go down and see what we can find." She smiled bravely at Kit.

Kit looked at her friends. They were willing to go down into an evil wizards' lair for her. She loved them for that.

An image flashed through her mind, of Alita crumpling to the ground as the fireball hit her. She pictured what might be down there, inside the crypt. A dungeon? The Dragon Masters?

"I don't think even Alita could squeeze through there," Josh was saying. "We need to push it farther open."

It took all their strength, and an extra spell from Kit, to move the stone door. After a lot of puffing and panting, they got it open.

"Wait," said Kit. Cold waves of air came out of the dark. It felt like the tomb went a long, long way down. She could see stairs descending until they faded into the darkness. She had a horrible thought: What if she was leading her friends down to die in the dark?

After pondering for a moment, she said, "We should make sure we're not disturbed. Josh, do you know a spell to keep people out of a place?"

"Yes," said Josh. "But it needs a closed gate. We can't do it on this tomb unless we shut ourselves in."

"Hmm," said Kit. "Let's do it on the gate to the

cemetery. It'll stop any evil wizards from coming in after us."

"Good idea," said Josh. "I wish I'd had it."

They hurried over to the tall gate of the cemetery and stood outside it, first checking that the street was empty. Josh told Kit the spellwords. "And you have to touch the people who are allowed through the gate as you say the final word."

Kit nodded. *"No permisso durch canhcong. Inside to you."*

As she said "you," she touched her own shoulder and stepped through the gate. It clanged shut and began to glow. Josh and Alita were on the outside, and Kit was inside.

"You forgot to touch us!" said Josh. "You'll have to do it again."

"No, I didn't forget," said Kit. "This is too dangerous. I need to do this on my own."

"What?" Alita looked horrified.

"I'm sorry. It's for your own good," said Kit, and she broke into a run back toward the tomb. Her heart was hammering. *I'm doing this to keep them out of danger,* she said to herself. *I can't let those wizards hurt them again. I'm a wizard. They're not. This is for me to do alone.*

She reached the open tomb, looked around her, and started to climb down the long stone staircase. *"Ina,"* she said, and a ball of light appeared ahead of her.

She went down and down into the dark. As she got closer to the bottom, she whispered the words to extinguish the spell.

Then she waited in the darkness. All was silent and cold. After a few minutes, she started to feel a little silly. There were clearly no evil wizards down here. What if it was just an ordinary tomb?

"*Ina,*" she said again.

She was in a stone chamber lined with wooden bookshelves. There were spell books and various magical objects around the walls and littering a large stone table. There was also a package of cookies on a shelf.

"I didn't think evil wizards would eat cookies," said Kit to herself. "Makes them seem less scary somehow."

"I don't know," said a voice. "I think anyone with an underground lair in a tomb who summons Dragon Masters from beyond the grave is scary, whatever they eat."

Kit whirled around in terror . . . to see Alita and Josh standing there.

"How . . . are you here? Did the spell fail?" asked Kit.

"No," said Alita. "We climbed over the fence." She was glaring at Kit.

Josh pointed to his once-white sneakers, which were covered in moss and grime. "Look at what you made me do!" he said. "Look at my *shoes*!"

"Wait, you didn't tell me the spell wouldn't stop people from climbing over the fence!" said Kit.

"Well, who would want to climb if they didn't have to?" said Josh.

Alita was still glaring at Kit. "Why did you cast that spell on us?" she demanded. "You're supposed to be our friend."

"That's why I did it!" said Kit. "I didn't want you to be in danger."

"That's not for you to decide," said Alita.

"But—"

"Let's talk about it later," said Alita. "They could come back any time. We need to look for clues."

Kit looked around. She realized, embarrassed, that she had no idea what to look for.

"Maybe there's a sign of where they're keeping the Dragon Masters?" suggested Josh. He went over to a bookshelf and started pulling books down and flipping through them. Alita searched a cupboard while Kit checked out the magical objects on the stone table. She was just wondering if any of them were cursed and would turn her into a toad if she touched them when she heard footsteps.

"Hide!" she hissed.

They scurried around looking for a good hiding spot. There wasn't much in the room, but they found a grate leading to another tunnel—perhaps to let air into the lair—and crawled inside, pulling the grate back into place just in time.

Three pairs of feet walked in. Kit wedged her face against the grate to see more of them. Three men.

One was the blond wizard.

"The masters are safe," said one of the others. "They grow stronger with every passing moment. Soon they'll be ready."

"When is soon?" asked the blond wizard. "That wizard won't be trapped in dreamland for long. She might raise the alarm. She might bring the council down on us."

"The spell says we have twenty-four hours before they reach their full strength," said the third. "Then they will give us our reward."

The blond wizard narrowed his eyes. "I say we kill her. Kill them all."

Kit's stomach dropped. *He means Faith . . . and us. And we're in his lair. Ready to be killed.*

We have to get out of here, thought Kit. *We have to contact Ben and tell him to hurry up and get the council to help us.* She looked behind her to the tunnel. Maybe there was another way out? That tunnel had to lead somewhere. And if it let air into the lair, surely it led to the surface?

New footsteps made her turn back to the grate. Kit could just see another pair of feet. The other wizards seemed to stand up a little straighter.

"Well, well, well," said a familiar voice. "What have we here? Evil wizards in their evil lair?"

Kit gasped. Ben! He was back! He was back from the council and they were going to be OK.

"Yes, Master," chuckled the wizards.

"Evil-ing all over the place."

Master? thought Kit.

"Quit calling me that," said Ben. "That's kind of the point of all of this. I'm not the council. We're all equal. I'm not your boss, I'm just the one who'll bring down the status quo. *The old falls. The new rises.*"

"*The old falls, the new rises!*" the other wizards repeated.

What is happening? thought Kit.

"But even though I'm not your master, I *am* coordinating our mission. So if I had to give you some feedback, colleague to colleague . . . you're really falling down on security," said Ben.

"What do you mean?" asked the blond wizard.

Ben sighed. "Have none of you noticed our three little intruders?"

Ben whispered a word, and the grate vanished. And with another word, Kit felt herself being dragged out of the tunnel.

"No!" she yelled.

Alita and Josh let out little yelps as they were pulled by the same force. With scrapes and bruises forming, soon they were all out of the tunnel and held in midair, in the middle of the room, in an invisible bubble of magic. Kit's body thrummed with someone else's magic. She couldn't get free. This was not good.

Ben and the other wizards were looking up at them.

"So," said Ben. "I suppose this is the part where you realize who's really behind all this."

CHAPTER 15

EVIL IS A MATTER OF POINT OF VIEW

Kit looked down at Ben, trying to make sense of what was happening.

"But—you're our friend" was all she could say.

Ben smiled up at her. The same friendly grin he always had. He even reached up and tousled his hair. How was this possible?

"I am your friend," he said. "I like you a lot, Kit. I'm serious. You're wild and free and impatient. I see a lot of myself in you. But I didn't think you were ready to know the truth. Now—well, I owe it to you. You've shown you're ready, by disobeying me when I told you to wait. I'm really glad you did that—I've hated keeping this from you. So let me tell you what's happening here."

"You're evil, is what's happening here," said Kit.

Ben frowned. "That was just a joke, with me and my colleagues. This isn't about evil. What I'm doing here is much bigger than that."

"If it's not about evil, then you wouldn't be hanging around with evil wizards and keeping us magical prisoners," said Josh. "Good people don't hang their friends in midair."

"Good people also don't bring back the Dragon Masters," said Alita.

"They've really done a number on you, that Wizards' Council." Ben sighed.

"No they haven't!" said Kit. "This isn't about them."

"This is entirely about them," spat Ben. "About how they held me back. Didn't let me use magic to help people. Didn't let me think for myself. But I didn't see the real picture at first. It wasn't until I worked on my powers on that island that I read more about the history of the Wizards' Council.

I read online about the communities of wizards who wanted to be free. I found like-minded people. We began to plan. Then the Dragon Masters came to me, and I saw a way to make the plan a reality."

"So you spent five years alone on a beautiful island, surrounded by incredible wildlife . . . talking to ghost rats on the internet?" said Alita. "Wow. What a waste."

"You're not getting it," said Ben. "The council wanted to keep me away from the truth. They refused to show me the magical texts I asked to see, just because they thought they were too dangerous! Who are they to tell me that?"

"So you went evil because you weren't allowed to read a book?" asked Kit. "Maybe I should keep an eye on Josh if anyone ever cancels his library card."

Alita snorted.

"Stop laughing at me when we're in danger!" said Josh.

"Stop talking!" snapped Ben. "Just let me speak. I can't think. Just let me tell you what I've wanted to tell you for so long." He put a hand to his throat, then gestured to them and said a spell: *"Shaanti hush!"*

Kit's mind was shouting. But her mouth was zipped shut, like her jaw had locked in place. She couldn't speak. She couldn't make a sound. She just had to hang there and listen.

"I don't want to bring back the Dragon Masters so they can rule the world. I want them to free it. Free magic. All these centuries, the Wizards' Council has stopped wizards from sharing the magic that could help everyone. Hoarding it. They stand for everything old that holds us back. We're a new generation. We deserve our own lives. Our own choices. We only want to share it with the world. Like, if someone had no food, we could create it for them. Or . . . if someone's about to harm someone else, you could do a spell to make them change their mind! What's evil about that?"

He was pacing now. The other evil wizards stood at a kind of attention. Then Ben stopped, looking up at Kit pleadingly. "You have to understand.

I didn't want to lie to you. I just didn't know if I could trust you right away." He looked at her. "Do you understand?"

He gestured and spoke a word: *"Shum!"*

Kit and the others gasped, freed.

"I understand. I understand that you're selfish!" said Josh. "I think you just want to do what *you* want, and pretend it's what's good for everyone else!"

"You just want to control people," said Alita. "You're saying you even want to control people's thoughts! That's disgusting!"

"Now, that's a bit harsh," said Ben. He looked genuinely hurt. "I'm not the only one who wants to protect others using magic. Kit here . . . didn't she just put a spell on you both to keep you from getting into danger? We're not all that different, you and I."

"How did you know?" Kit began.

Ben laughed. "I used a very special kind of magic. Called following you."

"That's rude!" said Josh.

"He's evil," said Alita. "Evil people are often rude."

"I'm nothing like you," said Kit. But she felt a little flutter in her chest. Doubt.

"If you say so," said Ben with a half smile.

"Anyway," said Kit, "how does unleashing ancient evil rats from the dawn of time help with you being free from the Wizards' Council and being able to make magic food for hungry people or whatever?"

Ben laughed. "I do like you, Kit. You ask such brilliant questions. Here's how it will happen. The Dragon Masters will bring down the council. Then we can form our own new world order. The old falls! The new rises!"

"And they've told you this?" asked Kit. "The rats?"

"They're pretty ancient," said Josh. "Why are they so into new stuff?"

"They're not part of my plan," said Ben. "It's just a deal between us. In exchange for bringing them back, they'll leave all wizards but the Wizards' Council alone. They just want to be free, too."

"How do you know what they want?" asked Alita.

"They came to me in a dream," said Ben. "They

asked me to help them, by throwing a bone into a lake. They didn't say why at first . . . but I found out. It was to start a chain reaction . . . ending with you using your magic to bring them back," said Ben.

Kit's eyes went wide. "*You* did that?"

Ben shrugged. "Obviously it didn't work. So, in my dreams, we hatched a more direct plan. And here we are . . . and they're back."

"And you trust them?" asked Kit incredulously. "You trust them to give you what you want?"

"I trust that everyone wants to be free. Deserves to be free," said Ben. "Them too. I just want everyone to be free—free from pain, free from hardship."

"You want everyone to be free except us, given that we're currently trapped in a magical prison," said Josh.

"That's only temporary, I promise," said Ben.

"What happens next, then?" asked Josh. "When the Dragon Masters have gotten rid of the Wizards' Council? Are you going to be in charge?"

"Not at all!" said Ben. He shook his head, smiling to himself. "All wizards should forge their own path, without the Wizards' Council giving orders. All I'm going to do is make that possible. I want to allow wizards to use their magic to help the world. Just imagine, wizards could cast spells to truly help people. They could cast a spell to . . . stop anyone who's about to hurt an animal! Or even just plant tiny seeds of goodness in everyone's minds, to make them just that little bit kinder to others. Wizards shouldn't be muzzled any longer. They're not dogs. They're not children."

"No, but we are," said Josh. "And we think your plan is a really, really terrible one."

"What gives you the right to use magic to control people?" asked Alita. "Don't you know how dangerous mind magic is?"

"It's more dangerous to leave all the power in the world in the hands of a few grasping elders. But I don't think I have any special right to do it. I just happen to be here, and with the will to do it," said Ben. "But now that you know my plan . . . "

"You're going to have to kill us?" finished Josh grimly.

"Not at all," said Ben. "I want Kit to join me. Help me build a new world. One that isn't stifled by old men and women who think they know best."

"I'm not joining you," said Kit. "Liar. Dragonnapper!"

"Just think about it," said Ben. "Let the idea settle. You could be free to use magic however you like." He turned to his followers. "Let's leave them. None of them have enough power to free themselves. We need to bring the Dragon Masters to full strength before we can finally overthrow the council."

Ben looked up at Kit once more. "Think about what I've said. We'll be back once the Dragon Masters are ready to bring down the council."

"Will they . . . hurt them?" asked Alita. "The council?"

Ben shrugged. "Frankly, I don't care. Don't worry about what happens to tyrants when they're brought down. Worry about the people they've been controlling. Come on," he said.

"What if we need to use the bathroom?" asked Josh.

Ben laughed. He made a crisscross sign and said, *"Hold!"*

Then he and his followers left the children alone in their magical prison.

CHAPTER 16

SOMEONE WE CAN TRUST

As the footsteps on the stone steps faded, they all relaxed a little. Kit sat down, feeling all the pent-up nervous energy leave her body. The magic hummed beneath her. It was a bit like sitting on top of a fridge.

"I can't believe Ben is evil," said Josh sadly. "He seemed so cool." He sat down, too. "I wonder how long this magic will hold us here for."

"I don't know," said Kit. She grimaced. "I'm sorry I couldn't keep you safe. Can you see why I tried to keep you out now?"

Alita, who was still standing, suddenly stamped

her foot. Kit shuffled back on her bottom in shock, then staggered to her feet.

"What?" said Kit. "What's wrong?"

Alita turned on her with furious eyes. "Don't you get it?" she said. "You don't get to decide what we can and can't do."

"I wasn't!" said Kit. "I was just . . . trying to protect you!"

"By taking away our choices?" said Alita. "Just like Ben's planning on doing?"

Kit gasped. She felt like she'd been punched in the stomach. "That's not fair," she said. "Ben was only saying we're alike to be mean! He's a liar!"

"Sometimes liars get it right, too," said Alita. She folded her arms.

"Josh, tell her she's wrong!" said Kit. "Tell her I was doing it to protect you both!"

"As much as I like telling people they're wrong," said Josh, "she's not wrong now. You didn't have any right to stop us from coming down here."

Kit swallowed. "But . . . it's my job as a wizard to protect people."

"No, it's not. It's your job to protect the dragon. Lying to your friends and making decisions for them is nowhere in the job description," said Alita.

Kit felt flustered. No one was reacting like they were supposed to. She'd been trying to save the day! Couldn't they see that? "So am I supposed to just let you get hurt?" she asked.

"No," said Josh. "We're your friends. You're supposed to trust us."

"You're not in charge. We're in this together, remember?" said Alita. Her face softened a little. "Kit, you're a powerful wizard, but you can be an enormous doofus. Now. Let's figure out how to get out of this cage."

They argued for a long time about how to get out of the prison. Kit had all kinds of ideas for spells that the others said no to, because they might "explode them all" or "turn them into Jell-O" or "leave them horribly scarred forever."

"For someone who wants to keep her friends

safe, you're pretty free and easy with the flammable magic," complained Josh.

"I, uh, want to keep you safe from other people. You're stuck with the danger I make myself," Kit muttered. "OK, let me try something less dramatic."

She tried a few milder spells, but none of them could get her out of the prison. Ben's magic was too strong.

"I mean, we could just try calling for help," said Kit, running out of ideas. "But I'm guessing down here, underground in a magical prison, no one could hear us. And if they did, it would just be a dog walker in the cemetery, not a wizard."

"Wait," said Alita. "Maybe we *can* get someone to hear us. The broadcast-the-quiet spell! Make our voices loud enough for someone to hear."

"Who, though? Faith and Greg can't," said Josh.

"How about the Wizards' Council? Or Duncan?" said Alita.

"I don't know if I can do the spell powerfully enough for someone to hear me in Scotland," said Kit.

"Who's nearby?" said Josh.

"I know someone who's nearby," said Alita. "Someone who loves me very much."

"Your mom doesn't know magic," said Josh.

"Not my mom," said Alita. "Someone smaller. And furrier."

"*DOGON!*" said Kit and Josh at once.

"Well? Let's do it!" said Alita.

So they got ready. Josh suggested they add a second spell to modify the first one, so their voices could be focused in a certain direction.

Kit performed the two spells, one after another.

Then they waited. And waited.

"I'm glad he cast that spell to stop us needing to pee," said Josh half an hour later.

"Is Dogon ever going to come?"

Finally there was a scuffling and flapping sound, and Dogon appeared in the chamber beneath them.

"Dogon! There you are!" said Alita. "Now you can do it, Kit!"

Kit focused on Dogon, reaching out with her magic beyond the bubble. She could feel the tingle of wild magic, the borrowed magic from Draca that had become a part of Dogon over many years. She felt the spell building, fighting against the bubble around them.

But it was no good. "The spell's too strong." Kit wilted slightly.

Dogon whimpered and licked at the bubble around them, then spat out its nasty taste on his forked tongue.

"What are we going to do now?" asked Josh.

Dogon whimpered again, then, with a flutter, turned and flew away.

"Dogon! Come back! Don't give up!" said Alita.

The children slumped and felt sorry for themselves.

"Maybe Faith will wake up and save us?" suggested Josh.

"Maybe," said Kit, but she doubted it. Ben had probably cast the spell on her to make sure she'd stay inside Greg's mind until the Dragon Masters were at full strength.

Just then there was another noise from the steps. Not Dogon this time. But not a human wizard, either. Kit felt a wave of wild magic.

And there, in the doorway, was the baby dragon, with Dogon bringing up the rear. Dogon gave a little barking roar as though to say, "Did I do well?"

"Good Dogon!" said Kit.

The baby dragon approached them, looking up at the bubble expectantly.

"May I?" Kit asked.

The dragon nodded.

Then Kit did the spell again, drawing on the wild magic of the tiny dragon, and this time . . . the

bubble began to melt,

and three children found themselves on the floor in a heap.

"We're free!" said Josh. "What do we do now?"

"I don't know," said Kit, looking at the baby dragon while Alita bent down to nuzzle and stroke it, hugging Dogon at the same time. "But I know who we can ask. Dogon, can you take the dragon back to the school library?"

CHAPTER 17

WHERE THE WILD DRAGONS ARE

Welcome back," said Draca as the three children appeared in the dragon's dream. Around them, the world was a dark, wild forest. In between the trees, hairy monsters were dancing and whooping. They didn't look scary. They looked like they were having a good time. There was also a small boy wearing a wolf costume and a crown, dancing with the monsters. Nearby, Draca was sitting on a throne, drinking some kind of potion.

"Don't mind the monsters. It's a story Faith was reading to me before she went away."

"Where has she gone?" asked Kit.

Draca tapped herself on the forehead. "Into his mind. Into his past."

"Greg's mind?" asked Kit. "So Ben was telling the truth? She's been sucked into Greg's memories? How?"

"An enchanted crown for the queen of the library," said Draca. The dragon didn't always give the straightest of answers.

"Oh! Ben did a spell on the crown before he put it on Faith's head," Alita interpreted. "To trap her in Greg's mind once they were connected by the spell."

"Sneaky!" said Josh, in an almost admiring tone.

"So how can we wake Faith up?" asked Alita.

"A problem shared is a problem halved. And a power shared is a power doubled. Or, in your case, tripled."

"Huh?" said Kit, unsure if she was misunderstanding some magical reference or if Draca was just being even more Draca than usual.

The dragon looked at her. "You'll have to find out what I mean as the plot moves on. No spoilers."

"Draca, has anyone ever told you that talking to you is really annoying sometimes?" said Kit.

"Many. But, of course, I ate them." Draca clacked her teeth together.

Kit was almost certain she was joking.

"I'm joking," said Draca. "Just in case you weren't certain of that."

"Phew," said Kit. "OK, so no spoilers, but *how* do we get Faith out of Greg's mind? What can we try?"

"Should we use a mind-magic spell?" asked Josh.

"Did you come to me for advice or to make suggestions?" asked Draca.

Josh coughed. "Listening now."

Draca breathed an amused puff of smoke from her nostrils. "Then I'll begin. Faith is wandering in Greg's story. Mind magic is dangerous, and she's deep, deep down inside another person's pages. Most magic risks pushing her deeper in. Except one magic."

"What kind? Illusion magic? Scrying magic?" Josh asked, beginning to list the types of magic.

"Not one of the seven," said Draca. "A magic that all magic links to. The story. You can free her with a story."

"You mean read to her?" asked Kit.

"Read to her, and then don't read to her. She'll come to you to find the end. A wizard draws her power from dragons, and dragons draw their power from words. Words can hook a wizard's mind like bait if you leave them dangling. Out of his mind, and into a story, then he will have his mind back. And that will lead you to the next piece of the story."

Draca stopped suddenly. There was a rustling around her. A pattering of paws.

"They're growing stronger. You'd better not dawdle. They'll be ready soon."

"But what do you mean, she'll come to you to find the end?" asked Kit.

"I've got it," said Josh. "Let's go. I don't want to wait until the rats come in here. Dream rats sound even worse than real ones."

"Then you haven't met the real ones," said Draca. "Go."

"Goodbye, Draca," said Kit, and blackness fell.

CHAPTER 18

A TASTE FOR COOKIES

"S o what was she talking about?" asked Kit as they left Draca's lair to climb up to the Book Wood.

"We have to read to Faith . . . and then stop," said Josh. "See?"

Kit didn't see.

"We have to leave her on a cliffhanger!" said Josh. "You know, read her something exciting and then leave her in suspense!"

"Oh, maybe we could read a book she's already been reading," suggested Alita. "Then she'll be really dying to know what happens next."

"I still don't get how that's going to wake her up from a magical coma," said Kit.

"It was something Draca said," said Josh. "About where a wizard's power comes from. I think it's because she's a wizard that it will work, because a wizard's power comes from words and books. Or, I hope it will work."

In the room where Faith and Greg were sleeping, Alita found the detective novel that Faith had been reading. She opened it where Faith had left a bookmark and began to read. When it got to a very exciting and suspenseful part, she shut the book with a slap.

Nothing happened.

Nothing happened.

Some more nothing happened.

Kit wasn't sure how much more nothing happening she could handle without wanting to bite her stubby fingernails clean off.

Then, suddenly, Faith jumped out of her seat

with a tremendous gasp. "What happens next?" she yelled. "And I need some cookies!"

A second later, Greg came to, more groggily. "I had such a funny dream. There were rats. And you were all there."

"You were in your own memory, Greg," said Kit. "And Faith was trapped there, too."

Faith was shaking her head. "Can't . . . stop thinking about . . . slippers," she muttered. "And . . ." She swung around. "You voted for *who* in the last election, Greg Daniels?"

"She had ever such a nice face," said Greg apologetically. "Cookie?" He passed her a package.

Faith took one, still shaking her head. "That was . . . something."

"You're both OK!" said Alita.

"I think so," said Faith. She looked around at the children, her mouth full of cookies. "You might need to fill me in on what I've missed. It's all still fuzzy."

Kit and the others started to tell her everything

that had been happening while she was trapped in Greg's mind. They were about to get to the part where they'd discovered Ben was behind it all when Faith and Greg gasped in unison.

"I know what was missing from the memory," said Greg.

"It was him! He was there!" said Faith.

"Who?" asked Josh.

Faith looked pained. "I don't know how to tell you this but . . . it's Ben. He was the one in charge of the wizards who brought back the Dragon Masters. The ones who stole the egg. And I think he's the one who put me and Greg to sleep so we wouldn't remember the end of Greg's memory."

Kit and the others exchanged looks. "Yeah, about that," she said. And then she told Faith the rest.

After a moment's silence, once Kit had finished, Faith made them all some ginger tea. "I can't believe it," Faith said. "He was my friend. He was a good guy, you know? Quirky, but good. He wanted the best for everyone."

"I think he still does," said Alita. "He just thinks

he should be the one who decides what's best."

Faith gave a sad smile. "I thought I knew him. But it's been five years. I suppose he's changed. I just didn't know he could change so much."

Kit didn't like seeing Faith like this. She looked like she'd been punched in the stomach. But seeing Kit's expression, Faith waved it away.

"I'll grieve the friend I lost later. Now we need to figure out how to beat the villain I've gained."

"And his evil wizard lackeys," added Alita.

"And don't forget the evil giant rats from the dawn of time!" said Kit with a flourish.

"Is anyone else mildly panicking?" asked Josh. "Or is it just me? Which means you're all super confident we can win, yes? Good? Good. OK. Good."

"Well, on the plus side, we have Faith back," said Kit.

"And I have you three," said Faith.

"And me," said Greg. "Ooh, my hip. I got really stiff sitting there for so long. Anyone got an aspirin?"

CHAPTER 19

THE BATTLE BEGINS

Without putting up much of a fight, Greg agreed to stay behind and guard the baby dragon.

"Stay and guard them both, Dogon," said Alita.

Dogon nodded and sat at Greg's feet. Whether that was because he was promising to be a brave guard Dogon, or because Greg had a large package of cookies, it wasn't clear.

They gathered up a few last spells and some magical objects from the stacks beneath Chatsworth Library and made their way to the cemetery. Josh memorized a couple of new battle spells, and Faith handed him and Alita a number of crystals.

"These hold stored spells I cast earlier so you can use them to defend yourself. Ideally, you'd have a few years' more training before you had to use battle magic," said Faith to Kit. "But remember, we're only holding them at bay until the council gets here. No heroics."

"No risk of that," said Kit. "I'm utterly terrified." There was indeed a huge and heart-sucking terror inside her. The Dragon Masters were awake now. They weren't at full strength yet, but it was only a matter of time. And Ben and his followers were bad enough. "So. Shall we go?" she asked. But for the first time, she was desperate to stay inside the safe walls of the library.

When they reached the ruined chapel, Ben was waiting for them, along with the other hooded wizards. They all wore cloaks of varying colors. Worryingly high-ranking colors.

Behind the group of evil wizards, the Dragon

Masters were lined up, frozen in place inside magical bubbles of force, like the trap Ben had kept Kit and her friends in, only these were glowing pink. Kit wondered what those were for. Faith saw her looking.

"That's to protect them, until they're at full strength," she said. "I know that spell. They'll glow green when they're about to release the creatures inside. All right. Ready?"

"Ready," said Kit. They walked closer.

"Hello, Faith," said Ben as they stopped, standing in a line facing the wizards. "This is weird, isn't it? After all these years, we're back together . . . but on opposite sides of a fight."

"If it's weird, it's because you made it weird," said Faith. "But for the sake of the years we were friends, would it do any good if I asked you to surrender? Change your mind? Help us stop the Dragon Masters?"

"I could say the same to you. Before the Dragon Masters truly rise, can I persuade you to change your mind? Come and overthrow the council.

Fight against the power of old men and women."

"Compared to me, you're an old man," said Kit.

"Hey," said Faith. "He's my age!"

"Last chance," said Ben. "Kit, you have such potential to help people. Won't you join me? Help other people live in a better world?"

"You mean control other people," spat Kit. "The answer's no."

Ben looked sad. "Then I'm afraid this is all that's left." He held up a hand crackling with magic.

"*Tortuga!*" Before the fireball hit, Kit had a shield up.

The blond wizard next to Ben hurled another fireball. It slammed against Kit's shield, weakening it. Ben raised his hands to cast again.

"Now, Alita!" yelled Faith.

Alita unleashed a stored spell from a crystal by rubbing her hand along it like she was stroking a cat, just as Faith had shown her. It sent a shimmer through the air that slammed into Ben and pushed his hands together. He tried to pull them apart, but they seemed stuck, like he'd gotten superglue on them.

"WOW! YOU DID A SPELL!" said Josh.

Spells flew back and forth. Josh freed the spell from his crystal to block a fireball coming from one of Ben's followers. It bounced the fireball back in another direction, melting it harmlessly into the air.

"THAT IS THE BEST THING THAT HAS EVER HAPPENED!" yelled Josh.

"*Shimmersphere!*" cried Kit, unleashing a spell of her own, capturing the blond wizard in a ring of sparks.

Even in the midst of battle, Faith gave her a proud look.

Kit's heart soared. Faith had bound another wizard in glowing ropes. Alita released another crystal, which threw another wizard back, pinning him against a tree.

They were winning!

Finally, Ben was standing alone against them.

His face was pale and his hair stuck up in multiple directions. His clothing was torn in places, and burned in others. He was panting to catch his breath.

"Wait," he said. "Stop!"

Faith held up a hand to Kit to stop her from casting any more spells. "Yes?" she said to Ben. "I'm listening."

"I've just . . . " He shook his head, as though coming out of a trance. He blinked and shook his head again, running his fingers through his hair like that would clear his head somehow. He looked horrified.

"What have I done? What am I doing?" he whispered.

Faith looked at him, her eyes full of concern. "Ben?"

"I see it now. I can see the truth. Oh, Faith, I'm so sorry," he said.

"I don't understand," said Faith. "What's happening?"

"I think . . . I think that the Dragon Masters were controlling me," said Ben. He wobbled on his feet, pale as a ghost, and looked imploringly at Faith. "Your last spell must have snapped me out of it." He looked from Kit to Faith. "I'm so sorry. I . . . I didn't know what I was doing."

"Oh!" Kit gasped. Of course! Why hadn't she thought of that? Ben wasn't evil. He was brainwashed!

He coughed and staggered. "They've . . . drained me . . . " he said, slumping forward. Instinctively, Kit ran forward to help him.

"Kit, don't!" came Alita's voice as Kit ran toward him.

Kit took Ben's hand to help him up. But instead of a weak grip, she felt her hand trapped in strong fingers. Then, with a whisper, he cast a faint spell on her, just enough to stop her from moving.

"What?" said Kit. "I don't understand. Are they still controlling you?"

"No," said Ben.

Kit felt herself spun around by an invisible force so that she was facing the Dragon Masters.

"They never were. But thank you for coming to me. You're a good kid," he said. Then, louder, he warned, "I recommend the rest of you stay right where you are." He traced his finger across Kit's throat in a menacing gesture. "All I need is time for the Dragon Masters to gain their last strength."

Kit felt incredibly naive in that moment. "You were stalling this whole time," she said.

"How could I not have realized," growled Faith. "I wanted to believe so much that you were Ben again. The Ben I knew. I'm sorry, Kit. I'm so sorry."

"Not long to wait," said Ben. His eyes were wide with excitement. "Any moment now . . . " He gestured to the Dragon Masters in their glowing bubbles of force. Kit could hear a bubbling, fizzing sound. The Masters' eyes glowed a fierce red, and energy crackled all around them. Bound by

Ben's spell, she could still hear Faith and Josh and Alita, and could see them shouting in horror as the Dragon Masters burst out of their force bubbles.

"*FREE*," said one.

"*AT LAST*," said another.

"*HELLO, KIT*," said a third. "*WE TOLD YOU WE'D BE BACK.*"

"So," said Ben to the rats. "What do you say? Time to overthrow the Wizards' Council and free the world?"

"*ONE OUT OF TWO ISN'T BAD*," said the rats. Each one twitched a claw, and Ben found himself hovering in midair, along with his fallen, groaning followers. Kit felt the spell Ben had cast against her melt away, and she was free again.

"*WE DON'T NEED YOU NOW. WE WILL DECIDE WHAT TO DO WITH YOU WHEN WE ARE FINISHED.*"

"But . . . we had a deal," said Ben.

"*THAT WAS THEN. WE PREFER TO LIVE IN THE NOW.*"

Ben went even paler than he was already.

"Well, isn't that perfect," he muttered.

"You never should've trusted those low-down dirty cheating rats," muttered Josh in his detective-novel voice.

"*HUMANS ARE A BLIP IN THE WHEEL OF TIME. YOU ARE BARELY EVEN WIZARDS. YOUR MAGIC IS BORROWED FROM BOOKS AND WORDS AND DRAGONS. OURS FLOWS THROUGH OUR VEINS LIKE WATER. WHY ARE WE EVEN SPEAKING TO YOU? PERHAPS BECAUSE WE HAVE LAIN SILENT FOR SO LONG. BUT SOON THE HUMANS WILL BE NOTHING BUT OUR SCURRYING SERVANTS. THE WORLD IS OURS NOW.*"

"*COME!*" said one of the rats. "*WE CAN FIGHT FOR OURSELVES AT LAST! IT HAS BEEN SO LONG SINCE WE FELT BLOOD ON OUR PAWS. NOW, FRIENDS, LET US DESTROY THE COUNCIL.*"

"I would really rather you didn't," said Branwen, appearing from thin air. The rest of the council popped into being beside her. "I have a lot to do today."

"Wow, are the rats powerful enough to just summon you here?" asked Kit.

"No, dear,"
said Branwen. "But
you are. We heard your
call when you were
trapped, but it took us
a while to get here."

"Because it's so
far?" asked Kit.

"No, because this
isn't the only Earth-
threatening magical
emergency today,"
said Branwen.
"Apocalypses are like
buses, I tell you. You wait
years for one, then three come along at once!"

Kit filed that away as something to wrap her
brain around later.

"Step back, would you?" asked Branwen, gesturing to the children to move aside. "Let us clean up
the vermin problem. I can promise you fireworks.
The greatest show on earth."

Fireworks was the right word. The Dragon Masters struck first. A single spell from many hands. They fought as one—just as they spoke as one. Magic came out of their clawlike hands in a glittering mist that seemed to swallow the council whole.

Kit couldn't quite follow what happened next. Spell clashed with spell, fire burst out, and shapes changed within a thick cloud of terrifying magic. What looked like a unicorn reared up one moment; the next, a shaft of green light shot up into the sky. Spells exploded. Magic roared. A wave of flame crashed over the battlefield.

"Stay here," ordered Faith, and muttered the words to a powerful spell.

"Faith!" yelled Kit as her teacher leaped through the air, eyes blazing with a golden fire, onto the back of one of the rats.

More fireballs flew. A volcano of light erupted in the sky, and the air split with screaming.

When the smoke cleared, one side stood victorious.

And it wasn't the Wizards' Council.

CHAPTER 20

MAKE EARTH GREAT AGAIN

Kit wasn't sure if the council members were alive, or even where they were. A tree stood where Branwen had been, in exactly the pose Kit had last seen her, arms out—only now they were branches. Several wizards lay on the ground, not moving. Some of the council members were simply not there at all. Faith hung in the air, suspended in a bubble of energy, with Ben looking up at her. His face looked half-sad, half-victorious.

The rats came forward on soft paws. They were whispering. Then they laughed. It was a sound as ugly and shrieking as a car alarm.

Kit, Alita, and Josh looked at one another. Then they turned and sprinted away into the cemetery as fast as they could.

"THERE IS NOWHERE TO RUN," came a horrible voice from behind them. *"THIS WORLD IS OURS NOW. OURS TO REMAKE AS IT SHOULD BE. WE WILL MAKE IT GREAT. WE WON'T MAKE OUR OLD MISTAKE AND WAKE THE DRAGONS. BUT WE WILL FEED ON THEM OVER THE YEARS. DELICIOUS POWER, OURS FOREVER."*

The children ran, pelting down a cemetery path. Alita stumbled on a root but didn't slow. There was no sound of the rats following them.

"In here!" said Kit, gesturing to a hut in a corner of the cemetery, which turned out to be the visitor information center. They rushed inside and shut the door. Kit cast a spell to keep it closed, hoping that it might delay the rats from coming in, even if only momentarily.

"Are they following?" Alita asked, panting.

"Not sure," said Josh. "I didn't want to look back. Too busy running. Ow. My lungs hurt."

Kit pushed her face up against the grimy window of the hut. There was no sign of the rats outside. All was quiet.

"What do you think they meant about remaking the world?" said Josh. "I didn't like the sound of that."

"I don't know exactly," said Kit, still looking out the window. "But I think it might involve dinosaurs."

"*What?*" Josh and Alita joined her at the window.

Kit pointed to what she'd seen. A very large, winged creature, wheeling overhead on leathery wings. "It's a pterodactyl!"

"Technically, I think that's a pteranodon," corrected Josh. Seeing Kit's look, he added, "But I appreciate that the relevant issue here is that it's in the sky, now, and not extinct like it should be."

"I think I'm starting to understand what reshaping the world might be," said Alita grimly. "They want to turn things back to how they were when they were first alive. Which means bringing back the dinosaurs and wiping out . . . " She looked at the others.

"Us," finished Kit. "Oh."

"We need a plan," said Alita.

"Hide in here until the end of the world?" suggested Josh.

"I was thinking more of a plan that ends with us surviving. And saving Faith and the Wizards' Council and everyone else in the world," said Kit.

"That's probably a better plan," Josh admitted.

"I suppose we could get Greg to help?" said Josh, not sounding like he believed in his own suggestion. The last time they'd seen Greg, he'd looked exhausted, and only interested in resting up and eating cookies.

"Duncan? The other wizard councils around the world?" suggested Alita. She reached into the bag she had used for her crystals. "I have a duradar for you."

Kit nodded. She quickly called Duncan. As soon as she started explaining, she could see him go pale. "I'll call the World Councils. You sit tight," he said. "Don't do anything, OK?"

"I won't," lied Kit.

She put down the duradar.

"We're not just going to wait to be rescued, are we?" said Alita.

"Obviously not," said Kit. "I just . . . can't quite think of a plan." She looked around the room for inspiration. Sadly the informational pamphlets about the history of the chapel and local wildlife didn't contain any hints or tips on overthrowing unstoppable evil forces.

"If we can find a way to get more power, I've got a spell I think could work," said Josh.

"How can we get more power?" asked Alita. "We could gather up animals, like we did with Duncan."

"I'm afraid we'd need double that amount of power to do the spell I had in mind," Josh said with a sigh. "Maybe even triple."

"Double . . . triple . . . hmm," said Kit. Something was tickling the back of her brain. She wished her mind were like Josh's—with neatly laid rows of information that could be plucked out whenever she wanted. Something was buried in her brain that she knew was useful. But she didn't know what it was, or where it was.

"Keep talking," she said. "It might jog something in my brain that's gotten stuck."

"We could ask Draca for help?" suggested Josh.

"Didn't the Dragon Masters kill a dragon back in dinosaur times?" said Alita. "Should we really get Draca involved?"

"No, but I think Draca might be the key . . . " said Kit. She was frustrated. It felt like when she had food stuck in her teeth and her tongue was reaching around to get rid of it. Only inside her head. What was it? Definitely something to do with Draca.

"Whatever we do, we can't put Draca in danger," said Alita.

Finally, the mental bit-of-stuff-between-Kit's-teeth dislodged. Draca. It was something Draca had said.

"Josh, what spell were you talking about that you'd do on the Dragon Masters? If I had enough power to do it?"

"Well, I recognized the words of one of the spells Branwen tried on them. It was a transportation spell, to send them back to the dawn of time. It almost seemed to work, too; she just didn't seem to be able to build up the right levels of power to do it."

"OK, OK. So if I have enough power, maybe I could do that one . . . " Kit nodded to herself. "Will you write down the words for me?"

"Already have!" said Josh, pulling out his notebook. "I copied it down as she was casting it!"

"What are you thinking, Kit?" asked Alita, narrowing her eyes. "Where are you thinking of getting the power from?"

"From you," said Kit. "Both of you. I mean, I'm not sure it will work. But it's something Draca said. You know how she never just comes out and says stuff. But she said that, when it comes to us three, power shared is power tripled. So maybe if I can somehow share power with you two, it will get strong enough to beat the Dragon Masters?" Saying it out loud, it didn't sound like much.

"What if it just makes you weaker, sharing your power?" said Alita.

"Well, to be fair, the Dragon Masters are so powerful that Kit at normal power is weak enough for them to laugh at her anyway," said Josh.

"Thanks, Josh. Have you ever thought of becoming an inspirational speaker?" said Kit.

"No, I don't think I'd enjoy that very much," said Josh. "I don't like crowds."

Kit and Alita both rolled their eyes.

"Anyway," said Kit, starting to pace, "I don't know if it will work. But Draca doesn't say things for no reason. I mean, her reasons are generally very confusing and weird, but she's always got a point when she says stuff to us."

"I say we try it," said Alita. "I wouldn't mind playing at being a wizard for a little while!"

Josh blinked. "Oh. I hadn't thought about that. So if you share your magic with us, we'll be wizards, too?"

"Well, as long as the spell lasts," said Kit.

"Let's do it! Quickly!" said Josh. "Quickly to save the world, not quickly because I want to be a wizard."

The girls exchanged looks.

"I think I know a spell that will make it work," Josh went on. "The sharing, I mean. I don't know if the plan will. I've never fought ancient evil rats from the dawn of time before."

"Well, I'm always happy to try new things!" said Alita. "Mom says it's good for the brain."

Josh quickly taught Kit the spell, and she spoke it out loud while holding her friends' hands.

We three meet again and each become
our own
Treble, treble, treble
A split from one to lay down roots
Racinate, racine, where the wild things are
I give you what I have to give
Until what is within you
Becomes what it was meant to be.

They stood in silence for a moment, still holding hands. Alita and Josh shivered.

"I felt . . . something," said Alita.

"Did it work?" asked Kit.

"I'm not sure," said Josh. "It might take a few minutes to—"

There was a loud roar from outside the hut and the sound of crunching and crackling undergrowth. Kit ran to the window to see what looked like a gigantic *Tyrannosaurus rex* crashing through the forest.

"I don't think we can wait and see," said Kit.

Checking to make sure that the dinosaur was out of sight, they opened the door to the hut and ran back down the path, the way they'd come. It didn't take them long to find the Dragon Masters in a clearing. The pteranodon soared overhead. More crashed through the undergrowth.

"YOU'RE BACK. AND MORE COUNCILS ARE COMING. I FEEL THEM COMING," said a Dragon Master. "SHALL WE END YOU NOW, OR WAIT UNTIL YOU WATCH THEM FAIL?"

Kit looked sideways at Alita and Josh. They looked just like their usual selves. Had the spell failed?

No, it couldn't have. Something was happening. Kit felt a tug deep inside her. It was her power being pulled out of her, through her veins and out through her fingertips and down through the soles of her feet. She felt suddenly very weak, like she was made of water that was flowing downhill, dragging her down with it.

"INTERESTING," said another Dragon Master. "PURPOSEFULLY MAKING YOURSELF WEAKER.

IS THIS SO THAT WE WILL PITY YOU? BECAUSE
PITY WASN'T AROUND WHEN WE EVOLVED."

Alita and Josh gasped. They began to glow.
Josh's eyes gleamed yellow, while Alita's skin took
on an all-over sparkle.

"SHARING..." said the Dragon Masters thought-
fully. "AS A COLLECTIVE, WE RESPECT THAT. BUT
ONLY IF YOU ALL HAVE POWER TO BEGIN WITH.
OTHERWISE, YOU'RE JUST MAKING YOURSELF
WEAKER."

"This . . . tingles," Josh murmured.

"This is . . . incredible," said Alita. She looked at
her hands, watching their glow.

"I don't think we did it right," said Kit. "I
feel . . . like all my magic is slipping away."

Josh touched his forehead and spoke the spell
word, "Ina!"

The light spell flared weakly and failed.

"Oh," said Josh.

The Dragon Masters laughed at them. It echoed
all around the cemetery. Kit glanced upward. She
saw Faith, trapped in a bubble of force, staring

down at them in horror and confusion. She saw the remains of the Wizards' Council around them, transformed and helpless.

"I'm scared," said Alita. She slipped her hand in Kit's. Kit took Josh's hand, swallowing hard. She just hoped they could buy enough time for the other wizard councils to arrive.

"Me too," whispered Kit.

"Me three," said Josh.

"Well, at least we're together," said Kit. "Whatever happens."

"Um, Kit . . . something is happening," said Josh. He motioned to his hands. They were glowing with a bright-yellow light. His palms were see-through, like burning glass. Kit felt a strange prickling tingle in her own hands. Squinting through the sunbright light, she realized she could see through her own palms!

"Same!" said Alita, holding up her own see-through hands. She prodded at her left hand with her right index finger. "Oh phew, it doesn't have a hole in it. It's just . . . vibrating."

"The transportation spell," said Kit quickly.

They spoke the words in unison.

Kit felt a force flow through her, through her hands, up to her heart, and out of her mouth as she spoke. Light began to build around them, flickering and flashing, like a growing storm.

The Dragon Masters stopped laughing. They started chittering: a high-pitched squeaking roar of fear.

"THIS IS NOT POSSIBLE. HUMANS ARE NOT STRONG ENOUGH. WE ARE UNSTOPPABLE. WE ARE FOREVER. WE ARE THE FUTURE. WE WILL MAKE THIS EARTH GREAT ONCE MORE!"

Then a light swallowed them, and they began to shrink, smaller and smaller. The pteranodon wheeling overhead was sucked out of the air, and along with the gigantic T. rex they all whirled and shrank until, with a great rush and WHOOSH of air—

There was nothing in their place. Just a burned patch of ground.

"We . . . did it," said Kit. "We sent them back."

CHAPTER 21

TREBLE TROUBLE

The three children sagged to the ground in exhaustion. Kit felt like her bones were melting with tiredness.

The tree with the outstretched branches turned back into Branwen. The fallen wizards rose to their feet. The lost ones popped back into existence.

"Well," said Branwen. "While I do like trees, that's taking it a bit far, isn't it?" She looked around. "They're gone?"

Kit nodded.

Branwen waved a hand, and the air around them

began to sparkle. After a moment, she seemed satisfied. "Yes. Gone. For good this time."

She sighed and slumped slightly, supported by one of her fellow council members. "We have to heal. We'll be back soon to find out everything that happened here. But . . . " She gave Kit a careful look. "Well done, whatever you did."

Branwen clicked her fingers, and the entire Council vanished.

A second later, there was a footstep behind them. Faith!

Alita and Kit rushed to Faith's side. "Are you OK?" asked Alita.

Faith nodded. "But never mind me. What happened? What did you do?"

"A spell to share Kit's power," said Josh.

"Treble, treble, treble?" asked Faith.

Josh nodded. "It turned all three of us into wizards."

"Interesting. I wonder why that didn't just cut Kit's power in three?" said Faith.

"Also . . . when does it start fading?" asked Alita. Kit saw fear flicker across her face.

"It should happen in a minute or two," said Josh. "According to the book I read it in."

But a minute passed. Two minutes. Three.

"I can still feel . . . " Alita said with a shiver. "The magic is still there."

Faith got out her thaumometer and held it to Alita, frowning. The end of the device glowed pink. "Ah," she said. "That's . . . unexpected."

She switched to Josh and scanned him, too. The thaumometer glowed bright pink again. "Very interesting . . . " Faith muttered to herself.

"Could the book be wrong about how long it takes?" asked Kit.

"A book? Be *wrong*?" said Josh in shock.

"Possibly," said Faith. "But before we find that out . . . Where is Ben?"

"He was trapped in a bubble of force, with his bad guys," said Josh.

"Like you were," said Alita to Faith.

"My bubble popped when the Dragon Masters were banished," said Faith. "So . . . "

They all looked around.

"Ben's long gone, isn't he?" said Alita, rolling her eyes. "What a coward."

"He didn't even stick around to say he'd be back for revenge," said Josh, sounding disappointed.

Faith looked into the trees thoughtfully. "We will have to watch our backs, though. And alert the World Councils."

"Oh!" said Alita. "We should call them! And tell them they don't need to come! And Duncan! I don't want him to worry!"

Faith grinned. "I'll handle that. You three go home and get some rest. You've earned it."

That night, Kit dreamed of wizards dancing in groups of three, and rats riding dinosaurs, and, because dreams sometimes don't mean anything at all, going to the supermarket to buy a cow.

She rushed back to the library to meet the

others the next morning. They went down to the Book Wood, where Faith was waiting for them in the common room, along with Dogon, who was gnawing on a dog chew.

"How are you all feeling?" asked Faith.

"The same," said Alita. "A bit . . . tingly?"

Faith nodded and frowned. She rummaged around in a cupboard and brought out three cloaks. One was Kit's—white with yellow at the bottom. The other two were all white. "Try these on for size," she said, handing one to Alita and one to Josh. "I want to see something."

After they'd fastened them around their necks, color began to creep from the bottom, all the way up, like water soaking into a paper towel, until their cloaks were bright pink all over.

Kit looked down and saw that her cloak had turned pink, too, though with the additional yellow stripes.

"That shouldn't be possible," murmured Faith.

"I don't know," said Kit, feeling a bit grouchy. She'd had to work really hard to get her cloak to

change color at all, and Josh and Alita had pink ones already? Not fair. "Josh and Alita always did tend to skip levels at school, so it makes sense they'd go right on to pink cloaks from white."

"No, I mean . . . pink cloaks don't exist," said Faith. "At least, not anymore. It's an ancient school of magic, based on pure, wild magic."

The children looked down at their impossible cloaks. Alita wrapped hers tightly around her, like she was cold.

"It might be why the spell didn't just cut Kit's magic in three. Instead, it tapped into the wild magic in the world, making all three of you strong," said Faith.

"Will the cloaks fade as our magic goes away?" asked Josh, looking a little sad.

"I'm going to have to consult the council, but the fact that you're still registering as wizards now . . ." Faith shook her head. "I think, somehow, the spell might be permanent. Wild magic chose Kit before. Now I think it chose all three of you."

"YESSSS!" said Josh. "I'm a wizard! We're all wizards! Wizard trio!"

Kit offered him a high five, which he missed.

Alita, on the other hand, burst into tears. Dogon flew over to lick her salty cheeks.

"What's the matter?" asked Kit. "Aren't you happy? We can all be wizards together!"

Faith watched and said nothing, listening.

"I . . . It was fun to try being a wizard, and doing that spell together . . . I always wondered what it felt like, but . . . " Alita let out another huge sob.

"I don't want to be a wizard. Not forever. I want to live my life and be me. I don't want to be someone else!"

"You're not someone else, though! You're just you, with magic!" said Kit.

"This isn't my magic, though! I'm part of you now," said Alita. "And . . . what if I get lost and there's no *me* anymore!"

"Alita," said Faith at last. "I don't know for sure, but I don't think that's how this is. I don't think you have Kit's magic. I think Kit just woke up yours. And you too, Josh."

"What?" said all three children at once.

"Alita, when you herded the animals up earlier in the summer, both Duncan and I thought there was something a little magical about that. And, Josh, you took to the logic of spells so well, I always wondered."

"So we were wizards all along?" asked Alita.

"In a sense," said Faith. "The magic might never have awoken in you without the kick start of this spell . . . or it might have when you were older. We can't know for sure. But I think this was all you. Kit was just the spark that lit the flame."

They all sat in silence while that sank in.

"I still . . . I'm still scared," said Alita. "I'm not normal anymore."

"Alita, you've got the world's largest, most terrifying dog for a pet and you think dragons are cute. You were never normal," said Kit, giving her a punch in the arm.

"Careful," said Alita. "I'm a powerful sorcerer now. Do not anger me. I shall become as beautiful and terrible as the morning and the night."

"All shall love you and despair!" added Josh.

Kit laughed. Her friends were weird. Weird wizards.

"So can we start training now?" asked Josh. "I can't wait to try out more spells!"

"Soon," said Faith. "After the council comes back for a debrief. Though we'll have to get the council to send a new school librarian to train you during the year, while I train you on the weekends."

"A not-evil one this time, please," said Kit.

"Yeah," said Faith. She looked suddenly sad. "I still can't believe that's what Ben became. He used to be so . . . " She shook her head. "But that's not your problem. You've all done something amazing. You saved the world! And changed yourselves forever. So perhaps you deserve the day off, to just have fun."

"Learning spells is fun!" said Josh.

"Fun outdoors. Or with your families," said Faith. "That's an order."

So the children did what they were told. Kit and Alita went to play at Kit's house, while Josh took a book on wizard training back to his house, which was his idea of fun.

"Do you mind? That you're not the only child wizard now?" asked Alita as they played a board game in Kit's room.

"Honestly?" said Kit, moving her counter two squares forward as she thought about this.

"Honestly."

"I thought I would. But actually I feel relieved. I was alone. And now I'm not."

"You were never alone," said Alita, taking her by the hand.

Kit smiled, and fidgeted with her other hand.

"Hey!" complained Alita. "Don't use me being a nice friend as an opportunity to cheat. I saw you hiding that counter under your leg!"

"Busted," said Kit with a grin.

CHAPTER 22

BEDTIME IN THE MORNING

few days later Faith summoned them to the school library after classes.

"What do you think it's about?" asked Alita as they headed down the corridor. Everyone else was filing out to leave, rushing and shoving. Kit felt like a salmon trying to swim upstream.

"Maybe they've got a new librarian?" she said.

"Maybe there's a new spell book?" said Josh.

"Or maybe it's a new apocalypse?" said Kit.

"I hope not," said Alita. "I just want life to be normal for a while. Or as normal as it can be." She looked down at her hands, as if she were looking for dirt under her nails.

Down in the Book Wood, the air was fresh. The trees had grown tall over the past few days. Kit noticed piles of old books laid around the floor, too, ready to turn into new trees. Faith had clearly been busy.

She was nowhere to be seen, but in the air appeared a sign, written in glowing letters. It said:

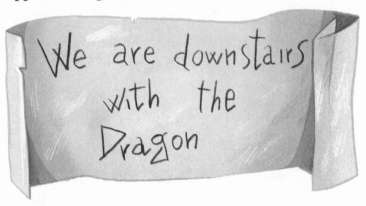

We are downstairs with the Dragon

"Which 'we'?" Kit wondered out loud.

They climbed down the staircase to the dragon's lair to find out.

When they got to the bottom, a large group of people was waiting for them.

Faith and the entire Wizards' Council were standing in a circle around the dragon's treasure hoard—along with Duncan, who gave them a little wave.

"Hello!" he said. "Had to come and see if you were all OK after the big kerfuffle. And it's always an honor to see . . . Well. What we're about to see."

"We're more than OK!" said Josh.

"They're wizards now," added Kit.

"I knew it!" said Duncan, looking at Alita in particular.

Alita looked away, but there was a hint of a smile on her lips.

"Enough youthful high spirits!" said Branwen. "We have something to do!"

In the middle of the crowd of wizards, the little blue dragon was looking around, curious. It let out a little chirrup and a puff of smoke. Dogon was fluttering around the chamber.

Each wizard wore a cloak. Branwen's cloak was green. The others wore blue cloaks, and Faith's was black.

"Your cloaks are here, children," said Iyesha.

They each slipped on their cloaks. Something in the air felt solemn, which kept Kit from asking one of the million questions she felt bubbling up in her throat. But she couldn't resist one popping out. "What's happening?" she asked. As a compromise, she asked it in a hushed voice.

"It's time for the dragon to go to sleep . . . and begin its real life," said Faith.

The dragon chirruped, clearly knowing they were talking about it, though unable to speak for itself yet.

"How does it work? Do we put it to sleep?" asked Josh.

Branwen gave him a scathing look. "It's not a sick dog. They'll go to sleep on their own. But we have one duty as it does, to help it settle in to its new dream life."

"Tucking it in?" suggested Kit. She wondered if you were supposed to scoop treasure over the little dragon to make it comfy. It was getting up and circling, then sitting down, as though trying to find the best position. It let out a little flaming yawn.

Branwen snorted. "Tuck it in? Think. What do librarians usually do to dragons?"

"Protect them from evil property developers and giant rats?" suggested Kit.

"Read to them," said Alita.

Branwen pointed to Alita. "Full points to the new wizard."

"Ooh, do we get points?" asked Josh. "How do we get points?"

Branwen sighed. "Faith, I don't know how you're not constantly exhausted by these children."

"It's a miracle," said Faith. But she was smiling. "Now, perhaps you three could do the honors." She produced a book, apparently from thin air. It was the first Danny Fandango book. "I thought you might enjoy starting with this one?"

"YESSSS!" said Josh and Alita at once.

The children read a page of the book each—even Kit volunteered to take a turn. As they read, the dragon's eyes began to sink closed. Its breathing grew deeper and slower. Before they reached the final line of the final page, it was deeply asleep.

"Come," said Branwen. "Let's join it."

Branwen knelt, ever so slowly, beside the dragon. The rest of the council joined her, then Faith, then Kit. Each laid a hand on the little dragon's flank. It was quite a squeeze. Josh and Alita went to hold Kit's hand, as usual. But she shook her head. "You don't need me now!"

With excited glances at each other, Josh and Alita each laid a hand on the remaining uncovered scales of the dragon's back.

Then everything went black.

CHAPTER 23

THE DRAGON'S NAME

The baby dragon was sitting on a throne on a pebble beach.

"That's the throne from Danny Fandango!" cried Alita in excitement.

Kit looked around to take in the whole scene. It was a beautiful sunny day, and a mermaid sat singing on a nearby rock. Not a real mermaid, covered in scales, but a storybook one, with a swimsuit top made out of shells, and long black hair. She waved at Kit. But Kit's attention was all on the dragon.

"Hello," it said. "Nice to meet you at last. I'm a boy, by the way."

"Hi." Kit felt shy all of a sudden. She was used to the dragon being a defenseless baby, with no words. But this dreaming dragon looked so much more alert and alive. And he could talk, obviously.

"How did he learn to talk?" Josh whispered.

"Those stories you were reading him weren't just to entertain him," said Faith. "You were also teaching him to speak."

"So everything I know, I learned from books they read me?" said the dragon. He frowned. "That explains why I don't know any jokes. You need to read me some more funny books."

"There are *many* books in your future," said Branwen, who was standing just behind him with the rest of the council. "Welcome, friend. We wanted to give you a proper waking party. Unfortunately, your own librarian can't be here, due to being an evil traitor who betrayed us all and ran away."

"That's OK," said the dragon. He looked to Kit, Josh, and Alita. "I have plenty of librarians to look after me."

The three children grinned. "Does that mean we get to run the school library now?" asked Josh.

"Not in the slightest," said Branwen. "You may be miraculous and unexplained wizards, but that's a job for a trained professional."

"Kit hopes you don't send an evil one this time," said the dragon.

Kit gave the dragon a look. "I think we need to chat about you not saying my thoughts out loud around important people."

"Sorry," said the dragon. But he looked like he was laughing.

Luckily, so was Branwen. "It's a fair criticism. Apparently our vetting has gotten a little slack recently. Whoever becomes your next school librarian will, I promise, not be plotting to overthrow the council and unleash a plague of evil ghost rats from the dawn of time. Or any other kind of plague. Any applications from people promising to unleash plagues will go right in the garbage."

Behind them, Kit heard the sound of large feet on the pebbles of the beach.

"It's time," said Branwen.

Kit and the others swung around to see who was coming.

"Draca! Draig!" said Alita. "And Dogon!" The little dog dragon was flapping around above Draca's and Draig's heads.

"We came for the naming," said Draca.

"Hello, little one. Are you ready to take a name?" asked Draig.

The little dragon nodded. "I know that it's traditional to call yourself by a name that means dragon, but I'd like to choose a different name. This is a time of change, isn't it?"

"What name do you choose?" asked Branwen.

"I want a story name. So I'll be Danny Fandango," said the little dragon.

Alita and Josh almost squealed with excitement, but everyone else was looking very serious, so they covered their mouths with their hands.

"Sleep well, then, Danny Fandango," said Branwen. "May your waking dreams be rich and full of life

and thought. May you be visited by good wizards and kind dragons."

"How does it feel, being asleep?" Alita asked Danny.

Danny thought about this for a moment. "I actually feel more awake. Like the first part of my life was a fog, but now I'm really me. I'm in the world

I was meant for. I can be anything now. I can go anywhere." The dragon looked around at Alita and Josh. "How does it feel being wizards?"

"I didn't like it at first," said Alita. "It scared me. But I've been thinking. Being a wizard means I can help protect dragons. And I love dragons. So maybe it's worth being . . . a bit different than I used to be."

"I just can't wait to start training," said Josh. "I hope Faith gives me lots of homework."

"You know what I can't wait to start doing?" asked Kit.

"What?" asked Alita.

"Correcting Josh's spells," said Kit with a grin.

Josh sniffed. "What makes you think I'll make mistakes?"

"Now I'm *really* looking forward to it," said Kit. "I might even keep a notebook with every single thing he gets wrong."

"Yeah, but you'd probably give up after a page," said Josh. "And fill the rest with doodles of butts."

"Only the dragons are allowed to read my mind," said Kit.

Eventually the party started to wind down. They said goodbye to Danny and the other dragons and returned to the waking world.

And then they said goodbye to the rest of the Wizards' Council in the Book Wood beneath the school.

"A word of advice," said Branwen to Kit. "Don't relax too much. Just because one evil has been defeated, it doesn't mean the world is safe. Evil is more like a game of Whac-A-Mole: another always pops up once you've beaten the first one. Threats to the dragons and the world happen all the time. More than you ever hear about. So stay alert. Now, I think I might use that lovely garden book to go back home. Prop it up for me, would you, someone?"

When the ancient wizards were gone, Kit, Josh, and Alita looked at Faith. "Should we start training now, then?" asked Josh. "Since there's all that evil out there waiting?"

"Evil can wait a night," said Faith. "But I'll see all three of you in the library after school tomorrow."

They nodded. They were ready. All three of them.

✳ A YOUNG WIZARD'S GUIDE TO ✳ BABY DRAGON CARE

Taking care of a baby dragon is easy when you know how! When your dragon is freshly hatched, make sure you keep them in a dry, comfortable place beneath your new library. This is where they will sleep and dream as an adult dragon, so make sure the cavern is large enough so they have plenty of space to grow. Then, perform a treasure spell to create a nice golden bed for the tiny dragon.

Next, make sure your baby dragon is not kidnapped by evil wizards. This is VERY IMPORTANT, as being kidnapped is very scary for a young dragon.

Before you know it, your dragon will be ready to go to sleep. Once they do, your role as magical caregiver truly begins! Here are some more very important tips to help you give your baby dragon the best start in life!

- Select their very first story carefully. A dragon's dream world is created out of the stories they hear, and the first bedtime story you read to your hatchling as they drift off to sleep will have a big influence on their life. If you want them to feel safe, try reading stories about happy baby dragons!

- Make sure to keep the library above EXTRA quiet for the first few months. You don't want a grumpy baby dragon waking up!

- Cast protection spells on the sleeping dragon to protect them from bad guys!

- Sleeping dragons don't need to eat, but if you toast marshmallows nearby, the smell will give them sweet dreams. (You could even toast the marshmallows on their fiery breath as they snore.)

- Read the baby stories that YOU love. They will feel that love through the words of the story.

I just know you'll be an amazing caretaker for any baby dragon lucky enough to have you looking after them!

✳ ᴀᴄᴋɴᴏᴡʟᴇᴅɢᴍᴇɴᴛs ✳

The world is strange and dark at the moment.
Thank you to all the people who make it lighter.
Karen Lawler, first and foremost. You are the only
person to see out a pandemic with. 10/10 would
recommend as an apocalypse companion. So,
like Michael Sheen, your name comes first. My
Lightbringer.

Thanks to my parents, for frequently dogsitting
Dogon.

Thanks as ever to Tom and all at Nosy Crow and
thanks to Polly Nolan for bringing these books
about in the first place. Thanks to my readers,
Ammara and Samantha, who help me see beyond
my own nose. Extra thanks to Az, my extra eyes.
You rock.

Thank you to Davide for what I think is his finest
work yet—and the rainbow wristband. You make
me want to buy all of Kit's outfits! I love how you've
brought the action and magic to life. And you cap-
tured Ben's hair so perfectly.

Thanks to the Girls, for all your cheerleading and welcome distractions.

Thanks to Team Swag. I couldn't ask for a better secret society. I am in awe of all of you.

Thanks to my Toots. Is black hole. Spaship.

Lastly, thanks to Shannon, James, and the rest of the Ladybirds, because you're awesome.

ABOUT THE AUTHOR & ILLUSTRATOR

LOUIE STOWELL started her career writing carefully researched books about space, ancient Egypt, politics, and science, but eventually she lapsed into just making stuff up. She likes writing about dragons, wizards, vampires, fairies, monsters, and parallel worlds. Louie Stowell lives in London with her wife, Karen; her dog, Buffy; and a creepy puppet that is probably cursed.

DAVIDE ORTU is an Italian artist who began his career in graphic design before discovering children's book illustration. He is on a quest to conjure colorful and fantastic places where time stops to offer the biggest emotions to the smallest people. Davide Ortu lives in Spain.